MEDICINE SHOW

BILL CRIDER

1941-

M. EVANS & COMPANY, INC. NEW YORK

B·2

Library of Congress Cataloging-in-Publication Data

Crider, Bill

Medicine Show / Bill Crider.
    p.   cm.—(An Evans novel of the West)
    ISBN 0-87131-613-7 : $15.95
    I. Title.   II. Series.
PS3553.R497M44   1990
813'.54—dc20   90-3672
                                                       CIP

M. Evans and Company, Inc.
216 East 49 Street
New York, New York 10017

Manufactured in the United States of America

9 8 7 6 5 4 3 2 1

For My Parents, Billy and Frances Crider

Chapter One

Kit Carson felt like a fool.

He always felt that way when he rode into a new town, but it was part of what he was paid to do for the show, so he did it.

One reason for his feeling foolish was simple; his real name wasn't Kit Carson. His name was Ray Storey, but the Colonel wanted him to be Kit Carson, and that was what he had been calling himself for almost a year now.

There was nearly always some self-appointed wit in every town who would point out that Ray, who was only twenty-three, looked to be in pretty fair shape for a fella that had been dead for ten or fifteen years. Ray would have to smile and go along with the joking, which he never found anywhere near as funny as the fella who brought the subject up, and explain that he wasn't *that* Kit Carson, that they just happened to be two people with the same first and last names.

Then there was his outfit. He had let his dark hair grow long, down past his shoulders, and it curled up on the ends. The hair was covered, on top at least, with a beaver hat. He wore buckskin pants and a buckskin shirt, both of them fringed.

He supposed that some people might have liked wearing such a gaudy outfit, but he didn't. It was the Colonel's idea of what Kit Carson ought to look like, however, so there wasn't any arguing about it.

At least he was allowed to carry his own pistol, a Colt's Peacemaker .45, instead of whatever it was that the real Carson might have carried. However, the Colonel had insisted that he wear a foot-long Bowie knife in a buckskin scabbard hanging from his beaded belt, just in case he ran into anything that needed skinning, not that Ray could have skinned it.

So here he was, feeling foolish again, riding into a little town in East Texas, getting ready to set the folks up for a visit from Colonel A. J. Mahaffey's Authentic Indian Medicine Show. He sat straight and tall in the saddle, which helped call attention to the outfit. He was well over average height, an inch above six feet, and people couldn't help noticing him, with his long hair and all that fringe hanging down.

In fact, he never got far into any town before he was noticed by nearly everyone who was out and about. He had just come to the first houses on the edge of this new place, and already there were two small boys and a collie dog jogging alongside his horse. The boys were both wearing straw hats and kicking up puffs of dust with their bare feet. The dog was barking.

"Where you goin', Mister?" one of the boys asked in between barks. He was the older of the two, probably about ten years old.

"Just into town here," Storey said. "I have some handbills to pass out. Maybe you two would like to assist me."

"Sure," the boy said. "We can help, can't we Tad?"

The other boy, about nine, said, "I guess so, Bobby. Ma won't mind, will she?"

"'Course not," Bobby said with complete confidence.

Storey reined his horse to a stop and climbed down. They weren't quite into the business district yet, but he could see some of the shoppers and loafers looking down the street to see what was going on. Any stranger was news in a small town like this one.

"My name's Kit Carson, boys," Storey said. He hated saying it, but the Colonel said it was important that he let people know. Storey didn't find it easy to lie to people, even kids, when he was talking right to them. On the other hand, he didn't mind at all the other lies he had to tell in connection with the show. He could lie to a crowd with no trouble at all. Somehow, it didn't seem like the same thing.

His name did not make much of an impression on Bobby and Tad. They were probably too young to have heard of the real Kit Carson. They wanted to see the handbills.

Storey reached into one of his saddlebags and took out a stack of the bills. He handed the stack to Bobby, who looked the top one over carefully as the dog sniffed around Storey's low-heeled boots. That was another thing he had insisted on. No moccasins, though the Colonel had tried for weeks to convince him to wear them.

The handbills were another thing that the Colonel put a lot of emphasis on. "You got to have good handbills," he always said. "You got to make an impression."

Making an impression was something the Colonel thought about all the time. That was why Ray Storey had become Kit Carson. It was why the Colonel's wife dressed up like an Indian, and why his daughter did the "Indian Healing Dance." It was why they had The Boozer with them, and why the Colonel spent more for the bottles and tins his medicine was sold in than he spent for the medicine itself.

The handbill was bordered on all sides with structures that looked like wigwams, alternating with figures of buffalo and war bonnets. The Colonel was partial to Indian themes.

At the top of the bill in the impressive script lettering were the words COLONEL A. J. MAHAFFEY'S AUTHENTIC INDIAN MEDICINE SHOW, and below that was a picture of an Indian woman cooking up something in a pot while another woman danced around it.

Beneath the picture were the words "Indian Miracle Oil, Relieves all Diseases of the Skin, including Wounds and Sores! Taken Internally, will Relieve Weak Stomachs and Flush the Kidneys! Good for Man and Beast. One Dollar a Bottle." There was a picture of a bottle, which did not show up very well, and then more writing. This time the writing said "Indian Vitality Pills, the True Gift of the Indian to the White MAN! Only Three Dollars!" No more was said about the pills, but Storey was pretty sure everyone got the right idea. If they didn't, the show would leave no doubt in their minds.

The show was described next: "The SECRETS of Indian Healing Revealed! Hear the Squaw Ro-Shanna as she describes the Miracle Discovery of Indian Vitality! SEE the Miraculous Secret Indian Healing Dance! FREE entertainment!!! Songs and Festivity!"

The Squaw Ro-Shanna was the Colonel's wife, dressed in a buckskin outfit that had almost as much fringe as the one Storey was wearing, but which had more beading and was much more revealing. The songs and festivity were provided by the Colonel himself. He played a fair banjo and sang songs like "Oh, Susannah" in a rough baritone.

The next words were the clinchers, however. "FREE Exhibition and Lecture on Human Anatomy. Women and Children POSITIVELY NOT ADMITTED!"

Sometimes there was really not even a lecture, because the Boozer was too drunk to give it. That being the case, the Colonel would provide a few words about the exhibit, which consisted of two colored posters of a nude female, front and back view. The posters were a bit disconcerting to some who saw them, since the woman was divided by a line from top to bottom and half-skinned in each one, in order to show her muscles, but no one had complained about that in the year that Storey had been working for the show.

"What you boys want to do," Storey said, "is to pass these out to all the adults you see, men especially. And there's one other thing. Tell them that the show starts at one hour before sundown at that little watering hole about half a mile east of town. Can you remember all that?"

"Give 'em to the grown-ups," Bobby said. "Show starts an hour before sundown at the waterin' hole."

Storey figured that was close enough. "Right. Now you boys run on and get busy. I'll see that you get a treat if you come to the show."

Bobby handed Tad a stack of the handbills and the boys took off at a lope, followed closely by the dog.

Storey mounted his horse and rode slowly into the town, taking his time, looking to right and left and trying not to overtake the boys. Each time he passed someone, he tipped his beaver hat, smiled, and wished them a good morning.

When he got to the center of town, he dismounted and tied his horse to the wooden hitch rail in front of Sanders Dry Goods. He always liked to start with the dry goods stores. They usually had a lot of women customers, and he knew that even in his Kit Carson rig, or maybe *especially* in his Kit Carson rig, he had a certain appeal to women. He carried several handbills with him.

He went inside, removing his hat at the door, and stood until everyone was looking at him. The pause gave him time to get a look at whoever was inside and to overcome the slight discomfort he always felt at beginning his remarks.

A short, fat man that he judged to be the proprietor was behind a counter, measuring material from a patterned bolt, getting it down to the brass tacks. There was a matronly woman in a calico dress and sunbonnet in front of the counter, evidently the purchaser of the material. Another woman paused in her examination of several cards of ribbon, and a third, somewhat younger than the others, looked up from where she was admiring what appeared to be a girdle. She was blushing slightly.

"Good morning to you all," Storey said when he was sure all eyes were on him. "My name is Kit Carson, and I represent Colonel A. J. Mahaffey's Authentic Indian Medicine Show."

He swept down in a practiced bow, practically mopping the floor with his hat. Then he stood up and smiled, concentrating on the women. He figured the man would be at the show anyway. The anatomy lecture nearly guaranteed it.

"I'm inviting all of you to attend our show," he said, stepping up to each one and giving her a handbill. He took care to smile into their eyes as he did so.

The younger one smiled back. She was short and dark, with black hair and eyes and a ripe figure that Storey appreciated instantly.

"Now all you ladies look perfectly healthy to me," he said, stepping back and still smiling. "But you never know when you might need something to put on a wasp sting." He turned his attention to the woman buying the cloth. "Or you might even accidentally stick a needle in your finger."

She giggled and looked down at the floor.

Storey walked over to the counter. "And I suppose that you must be Mr. Sanders," he said, remembering the name on the store.

"That's right," the man said. He had a fox-colored beard that was starting to go gray. "But you don't look like no Kit Carson."

Storey kept right on smiling. He didn't feel like getting into an argument, and besides, he was looking for Sanders's help. He didn't think the women would be coming to the medicine show; they never made up much of the crowd, and in fact there were a few of them in every town who would actively disapprove of at least two of the show's activities, the anatomy exhibition and the Indian Healing Dance, which had certainly not originated in any tribe Storey had ever heard of. Sanders was different. He was a man, and he knew other men. He would talk to them about things even their wives would not. The men were the ones the Colonel counted on for his crowd and his profits. It wouldn't do to make Sanders angry.

"I have to admit you're right," Storey told Sanders. "I'm sure the Kit Carson you're thinking about was a much bigger man."

Storey drew himself up so that he towered over Sanders by six inches. "They don't make men like that in these times, but I believe the Colonel's Indian Vitality Pills can make a lot of us more like that Kit Carson than we ever believed possible."

He tipped Sanders a wink. "They aren't called the Indian's greatest gift to the white *man* for nothing, you know." He gave Sanders a handbill. "I hope that you'll display this in your front window, sir, and let people know about our show." He gave Sanders and the women the details that he had given the boys.

"I hope to see all of you there," he said, moving toward the doorway. When he reached it, he performed his bow again and made his exit.

Out on the boardwalk he looked around. He thought he'd done a good job in the dry goods store. The women had gotten the idea about the pills as well as Sanders had, though he hadn't addressed himself to them or become offensive. They might let their husbands know. And if Sanders knew any men with Secret Sorrows, as the Colonel liked to call problems of masculinity, he would give them the hint.

Smiling at the curious looks of the people he passed, Storey passed each one of them a handbill, saying, "At the watering hole, one hour before sundown," as they took it.

Some of them were already clutching handbills given them by Bobby and Tad, but Storey readily gave them another. According to the Colonel, it never hurt to double up on things, to strengthen the impression.

Storey made his way to the end of the block of stores and stepped off the boardwalk. There was a church only a few paces away down the dusty street, and that was where he headed next.

Most people might have expected him to go to the saloon, which was on the other side of the street, diagonally across from the dry goods store, and he would go there eventually; but it was a proven fact, at least as far as the Colonel was concerned, that most of the men who had a Secret Sorrow were not going to be found in saloons.

They were going to be found in churches.

Why that might be true, Storey had never inquired. He simply accepted it, as he accepted most things the Colonel told him. The Colonel was a hard man to disbelieve, even when you knew him.

The parsonage was a neat frame house next to the church. It was freshly painted and even the yard was neatly kept, with rows of flowers planted along the picket fence.

Storey walked through the open gate, up the flagstone walk to the house, and knocked on the door.

He was greeted in a moment by a rotund man of about forty with a very red, clean-shaven face and a shiny bald dome that was surrounded, except for the forehead, with a fringe of close-cut brown hair. He was wearing a black coat and pants, white shirt, and black string tie.

"Reverend . . .?" Storey said.

"Stump," the preacher said in a rumbling bass perfect for lining out hymns or delivering a ringing sermon on the follies of sin. "The Reverend Lawton Stump, sir. And who might you be?"

"Kit Carson," Storey said, not feeling as guilty as he usually did. Hell, he *might* be.

"And what might I do for you, Mr. Carson?" Stump said.

Storey was, even on such short acquaintance, irritated by the preacher's habit of asking what might be or what he might do. He wanted to say that Stump might jump over the house, but he didn't. He needed the preacher's help, just as he had needed Sanders's.

"Actually, Reverend, I'm going to do something for you," Storey said, giving him a handbill.

Stump gave it a cursory glance. "I don't see how this is going to help me," he said.

"Not you in particular," Storey said. "Your flock. You see, Reverend, I know that you are privy to many secrets." The Colonel had taught him to talk like that. A year ago, he'd thought "privy" meant something else entirely.

The preacher nodded. "I suppose that I am, but I fail to see what that might have to do with a medicine show." His mouth twisted on the final two words as if he had bitten into an apple and found half a worm.

"It might have—I mean it has a great deal to do with it," Storey said with all the sincerity he could muster. "You see, I know that there must be a number of men in your flock who tell you of their"—he paused significantly—"Secret Sorrows."

The preacher looked at him blankly, but Storey went right on. "If you were to get them word about our show, and about the Colonel's Indian Vitality Pills, they would be forever in your debt. Tell them to be at the watering hole, an hour before sundown."

He pointed to the handbill. "Indian Vitality Pills," he said. Then he began backing away. "Thank you, Reverend, for your time."

He left the preacher standing in the doorway, looking down at the handbill. He would not be at all surprised to see the preacher himself that evening at the watering hole.

Back outside the fence, Storey waited for a moment as a buckboard creaked down the street. A virtually toothless man grinned at him from the seat, and Storey, grinning back, passed him a handbill. The man looked at the bill, shaking his head and Storey wondered if he could read.

Then the buckboard was past, and Storey crossed the street and went back toward town. He stepped up on the boardwalk and went directly to the Western Dandy Saloon.

Without hesitation he pushed through the batwing doors. It was cooler inside, as if the hot air of the day had not yet had time to penetrate. Storey was not really expecting to find many people there at that hour of the morning, and he was not surprised.

There was a bartender, a large, slab-faced man with a handlebar moustache, standing behind the bar and polishing glasses with a sparkling white cloth. There was a man sitting at one of the tables staring into a half-empty glass of whiskey as if hypnotized by it. And there was another man at a different table, but he was not exactly sitting. He was in a chair, but his upper body was lying across the table and he was snoring loudly, his mouth open.

Storey ignored the customers and walked over to the bar.

The bartender looked at him as if surprised to see someone entering his establishment at that time of day. He continued to polish his glasses. There was a long mirror behind him, and the long wooden bar in front. The mirror was lined with glass shelves holding bottles of various liquors, most of which were probably never requested by the patrons of the Western Dandy. A brass foot rail ran the length of the bar, and there were brass spittoons spaced out for the convenience of the customers.

Storey leaned down and rested his elbows on the bar and put a foot up on the rail. He laid a handbill on the bar.

The bartender looked down at it, continuing to polish the glass he had been working on. He was wearing a white apron as spotless as the polishing cloth. It was worn and patched and looked as if it had been washed a great many times.

"Medicine show, eh?" he said in a squeaky voice that was surprising coming from a man of such size. "Where 'bouts you settin' up?"

Storey told him.

"Hasn't been a show through here in quite a spell," the bartender said. "You ought to do right well for yourselves if you got any kind of a show and if your pitch doctor can give a good lecture."

"The Colonel's as good as there is," Storey said. "I'd appreciate it if you'd let me leave some handbills here for your patrons."

"Don't know as I ought to do that," the bartender said. "The owner might not like it. He'd be lookin' at you as competition for the business around here, I expect."

Considering that the content of Indian Miracle Oil, which was not really an oil at all, was about 15 percent alcohol, the owner might not be too far wrong, but Storey's job was to get the handbills out.

"We'll only be here for a day or two," he said. "We're not going to lure away any of your customers. Not for very long, anyway."

"Well," the bartender said, "maybe it wouldn't hurt if I just left a couple of 'em around. I expect the fellas here in town will be hearin' about the show without me tellin' them."

"Probably so," Storey said.

"How about buyin' a drink?" the bartender said. "Just to prove your good faith, you might say."

Storey didn't drink, not even Indian Miracle Oil. He left that to The Boozer.

"It's a little early for me," he said, reaching into a pocket and coming out with a dollar. "But I do have a little something here for you."

"I can't take no money for passin' out your handbills. The boss'd kill me.

Storey clinked the dollar down on the bar. "That's not what this is for. This is for information."

The bartender looked at Storey suspiciously. "What kind of information would that be?"

"I'm looking for a man," Storey said. "Goes by the name of Sam Hawkins. You know anybody by that name living around here?"

It was a question that he'd been asking for almost a year now in every town where the show stopped. So far no one had known Sam Hawkins, but Storey was sure that sooner or later someone would.

Hawkins was from Texas, Storey knew that much, and that was the main reason he had joined the show. The Colonel had told him that they would be covering the state "like a blanket, my boy. There is not a city or a hamlet that we will not be visiting to bring the blessed relief of Indian Miracle Oil and Indian Vitality Pills.

Touring the state with something like the medicine show was just what Storey wanted to do. It was just the kind of thing that would give him a chance to find Sam Hawkins without drawing too much suspicion to himself.

He wanted to find Hawkins very much.

And when he found him, he was going to kill him.

Chapter Two

The watering hole was just about what its name implied, a hole in the ground with water in it.

It was really more than that, however. It was a natural spring that bubbled out from under a mossy rock that was shaded by tall trees. The water trickled over the edges of the hole and down a little hill and ran into a straggling creek that probably wended its way to one of the state's rivers and then on down to the sea.

It was shady and cool near the spring, making it a fine place to rest for a couple of days, and there was a clearing on the other side of the road that was just right for setting up the medicine show.

The Colonel had already parked his wagon in the clearing, and he and Storey had raised the show's tent the night before. The tent served both as a shelter for Storey and The Boozer, should they wish to sleep inside, and as a place for setting up the anatomy exhibition.

The wagon was a testament to the Colonel's belief in making an impression. It was painted mostly white, but it had red wheels with red spokes, and the trim was all painted red and blue. On the sides of the wagon, in the same kind of script that appeared on the handbills, were the words COLONEL A. J. MAHAFFEY'S AUTHENTIC INDIAN MEDICINE SHOW in bright red letters.

The Colonel was justifiably proud of that wording, since the "authentic" was successfully ambiguous and could be taken to refer to either the phrase "Indian Medicine" or the phrase "Medicine Show." If pressed, that is to say, interviewed at the point of a gun, the Colonel might even have admitted that the second meaning could be considered far more accurate than the first, since to tell the truth he had never been acquainted with an authentic Indian in his life. He had *met* one or two, however, though he had never talked to them for very long.

The wagon was generally pulled by two lop-eared mules, which were now cropping the sparse grass under the trees. Watching them from where he was sitting in the shade of a tall cottonwood tree was The Boozer, whose real name was Albert Stuartson, M.D. It was still early in the morning, but The Boozer was already well on the way to becoming stuporously drunk, swigging occasionally from a bottle of nearly clear liquid that he held carefully in his right hand. He gave the mules a languorous salute with the bottle, but they did not seem to notice him.

The Boozer was not required to do any of the work that went along with the show. He was there simply to give it legitimacy. He was, in fact, a real doctor, with a verifiable degree and a diploma.

He had once had a successful practice in a small community not too different from the one where the show would soon be performed, but the rigors of the work were too much for him. The hours were impossible, and he got little sleep; he was expected to travel to visit the sick in any kind of weather, including rain and snow; and he was often paid very little for his labors. Sometimes he was never paid at all.

After a while, he began to drink to ease the pain in his legs and back from riding ten miles through a driving rainstorm to deliver a baby, or to help him get to sleep after one of those times when he had been awake for thirty-six hours straight and was so tired that sleep did not want to come, or to get him through one more day when he had to share the grief of some young man and wife whose newborn son or daughter had died in spite of all the doctor could do.

After a few years of that, it was as if he were not drinking the liquor any longer. It was drinking him. It drank his ambition, his spirit, and his concern.

It was the latter that took the longest to leave him. His concern had been one of his biggest faults, and though he had tried, he had never been able to develop the detachment necessary to watch with disinterest as one of his patients died.

As the drinking grew worse, his wife left him, and eventually he gave up his practice. All in all, he was much happier.

He smiled now at the mules, looking at them through the clear glass of the bottle he was holding. They were only slightly distorted by the liquid inside.

He leaned forward. "'at's the ticket," he told the mules, who looked up at him with only mild curiosity. "You gotta learn not to give a damn." He took a drink from the bottle and wiped his mouth with the back of his hand as the liquor burned its way down his throat.

The mules went back to pulling at the grass. They had heard the same advice more than once and had probably not been interested the first time.

"Life," The Boozer observed, leaning back against the tree. "What a wunnerful life."

He would most likely have given up his life, too, and willingly, had he not caught on with Mahaffey, who allowed him to drink but who refused to allow him to drink so much that he killed himself.

It was cool in the shade of the tree, and there was a slight breeze stirring the leaves. The Boozer no longer had to worry about a practice or about working at all. All he had to do was display his diploma and reveal on request or, as was more likely, on demand, that he had actual medical experience. And of course he had to endorse the wonder-working properties of Mahaffey's oil and pills. That way no one could accuse the Colonel of fraud; after all, he had the approval and recommendation of an authentic, certified doctor.

Many medicine shows carried along men like Stuartson, and most of those men had the same habits he did, though perhaps for different reasons. All had the same generic name of Boozer. It seemed to fit.

The name didn't bother Stuartson any more than it probably bothered the others who shared it. He just didn't care. About the only thing he cared about these days was the first drink every morning and the last drink every night.

And all the drinks in between.

In the show wagon, Colonel Mahaffey and his wife, the Squaw Ro-Shanna, were making up the day's batch of Indian Miracle Oil and Indian Vitality Pills.

The Colonel was a middle-aged man with an impressive mane of thick black hair, graying only at the temples. He had sun-browned skin and startling blue eyes. His face was virtually unlined except for the smile wrinkles at the corners of those surprising eyes and at the corners of his lips.

His title was not a military one, for the Colonel had not fought in the late unpleasantness between the states, having had no interest in testing his courage on the field of battle. No, the title was strictly honorary, and in fact had been bestowed on the Colonel by none other than himself. He always felt that a title made a good impression.

Along with the title he had acquired a passable Southern accent, though he had been born in Indiana. "No one ever heard of a Colonel from Indiana, however," he had once told Ray Storey. "I prefer to say that I was born in Atlanta, Georgia."

His wife, a petite woman with a remarkable figure, one that she showed to advantage in her guise as Ro-Shanna, was a few years younger than the Colonel, and her dark hair had not yet revealed any trace of gray. Her real name was Sophia, but she used the name Ro-Shanna in the show because there were very few Indian squaws named Sophia.

There were very few Indian Squaws named Ro-Shanna, for that matter, but that did not bother the Colonel, who was quite taken with the sound of the name, which he had made up. He was apt to change its tribe of origin from day to day. Within the last year, Ray Storey had heard him tell various crowds that the name was Choctaw, Iroquois, Apache, Comanche, Sioux, and several others. The one he was most likely to stick with was Iroquois, thanks to the slim chance of running into anyone in the South or Southwest, the Colonel's preferred territories, who was familiar with that particular tribe.

"I think we shall need a large supply of the Miracle Oil this evening, my dear," the Colonel told his wife. "I have a feeling that this is going to be one of our more successful stops on this tour."

Sophia was not so optimistic, but she knew that her husband was often right about such things. She helped him pour the ingredients from their individual containers into a wooden bucket.

There was the alcohol, of course, and a good deal of water. A hint of oil of eucalyptus. A touch of oil of cloves. Coloring. (The Colonel preferred blue, bluing being easy to obtain and harmless to man.)

The mixture was stirred with a long-handled wooden spoon until the Colonel was satisfied that it was well blended. Then it was dipped out with a wooden dipper and transferred to the bottle by way of a metal funnel.

The Colonel regretted the use of the funnel. He would have preferred that nothing but wood touch his mixture. Wood, he felt was more natural, and more conducive to healing.

The bottles were a dark brown, with the figure of the head of an Indian chief in full war bonnet impressed into the glass. There was no label on the bottle, but on the side opposite the Indian head MAHAFFEY'S INDIAN MIRACLE OIL were stamped in the glass. All in all, the Colonel felt that he had an impressive container.

When the Colonel and his wife were finished pouring up the oil, they began work on the pills, although in fact the pills were not pills at all. They were made from licorice, which the Colonel was able to obtain cheaply and in large quantities. The licorice was cut into hundreds of tiny pieces which the Colonel and his wife, and sometimes his daughter, rolled into the shape of pills. The pills were then put into a sack with a small amount of powdered eucalyptus leaves and shaken until they were coated with the powder. Then they were put into tins and sold as Mahaffey's Indian Vitality Pills.

Although they were advertised as costing three dollars per tin, the pills were never sold at all. They were given away, "Absolutely Free!" as the Colonel put it, with each purchase of a bottle of the Miracle Oil. The Colonel firmly believed that everyone liked a bargain, so he threw in the pills as a kind of bonus with each purchase.

He was also well aware that there might be some men who might not want to admit to being victimized by a Secret Sorrow, and such men would not want anyone to see them purchasing the pills. So he made it easy for them, by not requiring them to buy the pills. To get them, all they had to do was buy a bottle of the Miracle Oil.

The tins that held the pills were white with blue script lettering and once again the picture of an Indian, but this one was of a smiling Indian brave.

After all the bottles and tins had been filled, they were put into the baskets which would be carried into the crowd by Kit Carson, Ro-Shanna, and Banju Ta-Ta (the Colonel's daughter, whose real name was Louisa).

"There, my dear," the Colonel said with satisfaction. "I believe that should last us for the two days that we will be here in this lovely vicinity. Unless, of course, your own lecture on the wonders of the Vitality Pills is so overwhelming that we have to make up another batch tomorrow."

Sophia smiled. She was used to her husband's flattery. He flattered everyone, all the time. It was just the way he was, and it was part of what had made him a success as the proprietor of his own medicine show.

"I'm sure that if we have a big success, your own lecture will be the reason," she told him.

"No, no, my dear. I will admit that I can be persuasive on occasion, but it is your own lecture—not to mention that wonderful outfit that you designed—to which we owe the largest percentage of our sales."

Sophia blushed, though it was hard to tell that she had done so. She was extremely dark, and she sat in the sun a lot to keep herself that way. It was important to her to look as much like an Indian as she could.

"I believe that the dress was your idea, Colonel," she said.

"Ah, yes, but you are the one who fills it so admirably." He reached for her and drew her to him. "Although I must admit that I like you almost as well when you are out of it."

She laughed and pushed him away. "Why, Colonel! And me an old woman!"

"Old woman, indeed!" the Colonel said. "If that is so, why do I have to take so many of my own pills?"

"I never see you take them," his wife protested.

"There are many things you don't see me do," he said. "Nevertheless, I assure you that without those pills, I long ago would have ceased to function as a virile man."

Sophia doubted that very much, but she knew that the Colonel actually seemed to believe in his own medicine. It seemed to be a contradiction, since he was making the stuff up right there in the wagon, making it up out of nothing more than candy, really, but he always insisted on its efficacy, even to her. She suspected that this was another reason he was so successful in making his pitch to the crowd. It was much easier to sell something that you believed in.

"Where is Banju Ta-Ta?" the Colonel asked. He generally referred to everyone involved in the show by their assumed names.

"Setting up the anatomy exhibition, I believe. Or she might be practicing her dance."

"Good. I'm certain that this is going to be a successful stop. I can feel it in my bones.

Sophia hoped that her husband was right. For some reason she had almost the opposite feeling, almost a feeling of foreboding, but she would never have said so. Her husband was a man with a positive attitude. He did not like to hear contrary opinions, so she seldom gave him one.

Instead, she simply smiled and said, "I'm sure you're right, Colonel. I'm sure we'll have a great success this time."

Louisa Mahaffey had arranged the two pictures for the anatomy exhibition in the tent, and now she was taking a walk through the trees near the clearing. It was a warm day, and she enjoyed the shade and the breeze and the songs of the birds, though her thoughts were more concerned with things other than her surroundings.

She was nearly eighteen years old, and a great deal of her life had been spent in the medicine show. It was actually unusual for women to be involved in such endeavors, but the Colonel liked to have his family around him, and both his wife and daughter had proved to have the necessary talent to help him sell his concoctions.

Louisa could vaguely remember a time when she had lived in a house all year round and when her father had been only an occasional visitor there, but that had been a long time ago. As soon as she was deemed old enough, she was taken on the road and the show wagon had become her home for most of the year. There was still a regular house for the worst of the winter months, when the Colonel preferred not to travel, but Louisa regarded those months as wasted time. She liked traveling around the country, seeing new places, meeting all kinds of people, much more than she liked sitting by a fire while her mother patiently taught her reading and arithmetic.

Last winter had been a particularly good one, with hardly any cold weather. Her father had taken advantage of the unusual circumstances to stay on the road almost the entire year. They had made a great deal of money.

Another reason Louisa liked staying on the road was that she got to be around Ray Storey that much more. It was true that he hardly ever noticed her, and it was true that when he did notice her he saw her only as a girl who worked for the show and occasionally got in his way, but she was determined that sooner or later he would see her in a different light. There had been a time or two lately, during the Healing Dance, when she thought she detected a note of actual interest in his eyes.

And why shouldn't there be? There was certainly plenty of interest in the eyes of the other men who crowded around the small raised platform when she performed. It was an interest that she had grown accustomed to over the past five years, the time that she had been doing the dance, and it galled her that Ray Storey seemed to be the only one who never noticed her.

Well, that wasn't strictly true. The Boozer never seemed to notice her either, but he was an old man and his senses were so dulled by the alcohol he drank it was doubtful that he would have noticed Salome doing her dance of the seven veils. Louisa didn't mind if *he* didn't notice her. She didn't even want him to.

But Ray Storey was different. Ever since he had joined the show, she had tried in one way or another to get his attention, without success. He was always polite, always courteous, but it was almost as if she didn't exist as far as he was concerned. He was that way about a lot of things. There was an air of preoccupation about him that she could never penetrate.

She had once talked to her father about it, but all he said was that "all men have their Secret Sorrows," and shook his head sadly. She was sure then that the Colonel had no more idea about Storey's secret than she herself did. One thing she was sure of, and that was that whatever the secret was, it had nothing to do with the kind of Sorrows that the Colonel's pills were supposed to cure.

She had talked to her mother too, but without finding any more satisfaction in her answers. "He may be brooding over a lost love," Sophia said, shaking her head sadly as the Colonel had done.

Louisa was convinced that he mother's notion was just as wrong as her father's. There was just no way that any woman was going to let a man like Ray Storey get away from her, much less jilt him and cause him to brood.

She resolved to put just a little bit more energy into her dance that evening. Sooner or later, Ray was going to be forced to notice her. She knew that the Healing Dance had done a good deal more for relieving the Secret Sorrows of a good many of the audience than a whole tin of the Indian Vitality Pills.

That, of course, was the point.

"I want those men to go home feeling as if they have received a certain amount of stimulation from our show," was the way the Colonel usually put it. "There will be the intellectual stimulation of the anatomy lecture, and of my own talk, but at the same time we want them to receive the more subtle stimulation of Ro-Shanna's description of the virtues of those wonderful pills."

What he meant was that the men would be stimulated by Ro-Shanna's outfit, but he would never put it that way.

"And there is also the Healing Dance," he would say. "There should be a certain sinuosity of the motions that will suggest to the audience the lithe sinuosity that their own bodies will experience when they have partaken of our marvelous remedies."

Louisa thought that she knew what that meant, too. She tried to make the dance as sinuous as possible, and tonight she would do even better than usual. Storey would be forced to look at her. And he would really see her for a change. Or so she hoped.

She saw that she had strayed quite a distance from the tent, and she turned back. Her parents didn't like for her to go wandering off too far. She was still young, after all, and you could never tell what you might encounter in the woods, or even in town.

She wasn't worried, however. She regarded herself as practically grown and certainly capable of taking care of herself in virtually any situation that arose, short of something that might involve shooting.

She looked at the ground, admiring the way the sunshine filtered through the trees and made patterns on the dirt. She scuffed her feet through the pine needles and thought some more about Ray Storey. She thought about his arms around her, pulling her close to him.

She was suddenly warmer than the day would seem to have warranted, so she turned her thoughts to other things and walked faster. It was time to get back to business.

Chapter Three

The snoring man spluttered awake and sat bolt upright in his chair, staring wide-eyed around the saloon. It was as if the name of Sam Hawkins had frightened him even in his sleep. From halfway across the room, Storey could see that the man's eyes were bloodshot and that he needed a shave.

The man looked blankly at Storey and the bartender, but it was plain that he didn't really see them. After a second or two, his head fell back to the table top, hitting it with an audible thump. Within seconds he was snoring again. The solitary drinker never even looked up.

The bartender put down the glass he was working on and stuck the towel somewhere under the bar. "Sam Hawkins," he said. "I guess that's a pretty common name."

"They call him 'Hawk,'" Storey said.

The bartender nodded as if Storey had said something with which he agreed. There was a strange look in his eyes. "He got a brother named Ben?"

Storey felt a sharp thrill shoot through him as if he'd been struck by a lightning bolt, but his face showed nothing.

"Yeah," he said. "That's his brother, all right."

"They ain't the most agreeable folks in town," the bartender said. He was talking in a low voice now, hardly above a whisper. "You might say they got pretty bad reputations."

"Sounds like the ones I'm looking for," Storey said. It was all he could do to keep himself from reaching for his pistol. He wanted to feel the comforting weight of it in his hand.

"Tough fellas," the bartender said, looking at Storey out of the corners of his eyes. "What was it you wanted with them two, anyway?"

"Just wanted to talk to them," Storey said. "We have some friends in common."

"Didn't know those boys had any friends," the bartender said. He reached under the bar and brought out a bottle and a sparkling clean glass. "You sure you don't want a drink?"

"I'm sure," Storey told him. "You go ahead without me, if you want to."

"Don't mind if I do," the bartender said. He pulled the cork from the bottle and poured himself a drink. The hand holding the bottle shook slightly, and the neck of the bottle clinked against the top of the glass.

"The Hawkins brothers live around here, do they?" Storey said.

The bartender licked his lips and brought up the glass. He put it to his mouth and leaned his head back as he drank, and his Adam's apple bobbed up and down. He set the glass down on the bar and wiped his mouth.

"Ahhh," he said, shaking his head. "I don't generally drink, you know. Too much temptation, havin' it around all the time. A bartender that takes to drinkin' don't usually last long in the job. But I needed that one."

"You know Sam and Ben, I take it?" Storey said.

The bartender did not answer directly. He reached under the bar for another cloth and started polishing the bar. The bar was so shiny that Storey could see his face reflected in it. It did not need polishing.

Storey waited silently.

Finally the bartender looked up at him. "Look, mister," he said, "I don't know you. You come in here in some kind of funny-lookin' outfit and say you're with a medicine show, and maybe you are. But then you start talkin' about the Hawkins brothers. How do I know you ain't the law?"

Storey laughed shortly. "You ever see a lawman dressed like this?"

That got a thin smile from the bartender. "No, I surely never did. I guess you're with a medicine show, right enough."

"I don't want to arrest the Hawkins brothers," Storey said. "I can promise you that." It was true. He just wanted to kill Sam Hawkins. While he was at it, he might as well kill Ben, too. Do the world a favor.

"I got to live here," the bartender said. "If it got out that I told a lawman about those boys, well, I might as well buy my coffin box right now. Those two—" he stopped and looked around as if there might be someone listening "—they'd just as soon kill a man because they don't like his looks, much less a man that sicced the law on 'em."

"Sounds like the men I'm looking for," Storey said.

"Friends of yours, you said. You don't look like the kind of friend they'd have, if they had any friends."

"Friends might not be exactly the right word. I know them, though. From 'way back."

"Listen," the bartender said, grabbing Storey's arm. "I hope I didn't offend you, the way I talked about 'em. I hope you won't be tellin' 'em what I said."

"No," Storey said. "I won't be telling them that."

The bartender relaxed his grip. "They got ever'body in this town cowed down. They make us dance to whatever tune they decide to play."

"I imagine they do," Storey said. As he had said, he knew the Hawkins brothers from 'way back. He straightened up from the bar. The dollar he had put down was still there, right beside the glass the bartender had drunk from.

"You never said where they lived," he said.

"Out in the woods north of town," the bartender told him. "You sure you want to go lookin' for 'em?"

"Oh yeah," Storey said. "I'm sure, all right."

Naomi Stump was thinking about Ray Storey as she walked back home, but she was thinking of him as Kit Carson. My, he had been tall and handsome in that buckskin outfit he was wearing in the store. She had almost forgotten what it was that she had gone there to purchase, just looking at him. She thought again about the way he had smiled at her, and her stomach felt weak.

She went into the house by the back way and was surprised to see her husband sitting at the kitchen table.

"I thought you would be at the church," she said.

He looked up at her, as if startled. Then she noticed that there was something lying on the table. It was one of the handbills that Kit Carson had been passing out, and it appeared that her husband had been studying it.

"Are you going to the medicine show?" she said.

He stood up hurriedly, kicking back the chair he had been sitting in, and stuffed the handbill into the pocket of his black coat.

"I might have to go," he said. "But only as the watchdog of the community's morals. I believe that such shows are often of a kind not conducive to proper behavior."

Naomi listened to the warmth of his deep voice, a voice that she had fallen in love with two years before, and wondered how such a sensitive voice could come from such a hollow shell.

She blamed only herself for her mistake. She had led a sheltered life until meeting the Reverend Stump when he came to preach a revival at the small church where her family were all members, and she had been completely won over by his preaching, his singing, and his apparent relish for life. He had responded to her in kind, and before he left they were engaged. He had his own church, and he was well able to support a wife.

25

After their marriage, however, she had learned that supporting a wife was about all that interested him as far as marriage was concerned. There were other things that she had expected, but they had not developed. At first she had told herself that she was sinful for even wanting them, but she knew that other women experienced them. She had heard women talk. She thought about the way she had felt when Kit Carson smiled at her.

"I'm sure there is nothing wrong with the show," she said. "I met one of the members of their party at the store. He seemed like a fine young man. I would like to go myself."

The preacher seemed to swell. "I forbid it," he said. "It would not be fitting for the minister's wife to attend such a show."

He pulled the crumpled handbill from his pocket and showed her the last line: "Women and Children POSITIVELY NOT ADMITTED!"

"But that refers only to the anatomy exhibition," she protested. "I was not thinking about attending that."

"I forbid you to go to any part of it," Stump said. "That is my final word on the matter." He stalked to the front of the house, looking for his hat. When he found it, he settled it on his head and went out the front door.

Naomi heard the door shut behind him. She pulled her own copy of the handbill from her purse and looked at it again. She read the part about the Indian Vitality Pills again. Might they not be exactly what her husband needed? She was sure that there was something lacking in him, and maybe the pills would help.

She thought again of Kit Carson. She was sure that such a man as that did not need any pills. He would know exactly what to do with a woman if he had her.

She decided then and there that she would attend the show, no matter what her husband had said. And she would buy the pills, too. Getting her husband to take them was another matter, but she would worry about that later.

The Reverend Stump walked to the church, his face burning, and not from the heat of the day. He could imagine what his wife was thinking. She was thinking that he was less than a man.

And she was right, he was convinced of that. He should never have married her, but he had been captivated by her innocence and her beauty and allowed himself to give in to urges that he felt were better ignored, or if ignoring them was impossible, crushed.

He believed that such urges were unbecoming in a man of God. He had fought them for years, successfully, he was proud to say. But Naomi had brought them out so strongly that he had lost control of himself and given in to them.

Not completely. He had avoided taking pleasure in the act, thank God, but it had been difficult. Almost impossible. He had tried to explain things to Naomi, but he knew that she didn't understand. How could she? She had not committed herself to living a godly life as he had at an early age. She thought that her marriage should be like everyone else's. But he had promised God that he would devote all his energies to the church, shunning the temptations of the world, the flesh, and the devil; he had to keep his promise.

He entered the church, and as always he felt an immediate sense of peace and relief. His face cooled. The church had been shut up all night and the day's heat had not yet invaded it. There was one window near the front that still had a small amount of stained glass in it, and the sun shone through it, throwing a pattern of red and green across the altar.

The Reverend Stump walked down the aisle, looking to right and left at the empty pews. When he got to the altar, he knelt down and began praying aloud.

"Forgive me, Father," he said. "Forgive my weakness and my human frailty. I know that I can do all things through you, if you give me the strength."

Usually he found it quite easy to pray. The silence of the church, the beauty of the mornings, the peaceful serenity of the old building, all aided him in his devotions.

But today was different. He found his mind wandering to the handbill that was still stuffed in his pocket. He wondered about the anatomy lecture, the healing dance, the Vitality Pills.

It was almost as if the right side of his coat were sagging down under a heavy weight, as if the handbill were pulling it earthward.

Stump felt his face growing hot again and he screwed his eyes shut tight as if that would chase the thoughts from his head.

But the thoughts would not leave him. Finally he stood up and went to the small room in the rear of the church that served as his office. He would work on his sermon for the coming week. That would drive the thoughts away, he was sure.

In the office, which was a room containing a writing desk, a chair, and bookshelves holding his bible and the few commentaries he owned, he began thinking about a text. There was a single window in the room, and he could see his ghostly reflection in the glass.

"If thine right eye offend thee," he said to the reflection, "pluck it out."

He took a piece of paper from the desk, dipped a pen nib in ink, and began to write.

There were no customers in Barclay Sander's dry goods store at the moment, and he took advantage of the few minutes he had to spare to look at the handbill given to him by the stranger who called himself Kit Carson.

Kit Carson, my foot, Sanders thought as he looked over the bill. He could remember at least one other advance man for a medicine show who had called himself the same thing. It seemed to be a popular name with men like that. That had been five years or so ago, Sanders recalled.

That show had been a good one, though he would not have admitted that to the stranger. Sanders secretly enjoyed going to medicine shows, even if he had no faith at all in the so-called remedies they sold.

In fact, he saw that the handbill was carefully worded so that Colonel Mahaffey did not even claim that his nostrums were remedies. He merely said they "relieved" certain symptoms, not that they cured them.

Sanders thought he would probably buy a bottle of the oil, anyway. The entertainment might be worth a dollar, and besides, he wanted to see that anatomy exhibition—any presentation from which women and children were excluded sounded as if it had promise.

He was putting the bill in the window where it could be seen from the boardwalk when he saw Carl Gary looking at it through the glass. Gary moved away from the window and came into the store. He owned the Western Dandy saloon and was considered one of the community's leading citizens.

He was a dapper man, thin and trim, with a shadow of a mustache on his handsome face. He wore a broadcloth suit and the shiniest boots in town.

"Mornin', Mr. Gary," Sanders said. "What can I do for you today?"

"Noticed the bill you were putting in the window," Gary said. He had such a smooth voice there were people who said he must drink honey for breakfast. "I was wondering what you knew about the show."

"Nothin' much," Sanders said. "The advance man just left it with me. All I know's what's on the paper."

Gary reached into the window and took the handbill. Sanders did not protest. He simply stood there in silence while Gary read it.

"No harm in it that I can see," Gary said when he was finished. "I'm sure the fellow is a fraud, but he might bring a bit of entertainment to the town. Nothing wrong with that, I suppose."

"No, sir, nothin' wrong with that," Sanders said. "That's exactly what I was thinkin' myself. You goin' to the show, then?"

"Probably not," Gary said. "I have other things to attend to. Good day, Mr. Sanders." He turned his back on the storekeeper and walked out the door.

Uppity bastard, Sanders thought. Too good to go to a show with the common folks.

Gary was not one of Sanders's favorite people. He might be a wealthy man, but he thought he was better than everybody else when he really wasn't. He was just richer, that was all. Sanders wondered how long Gary's wealth would last. If the Hawkins brothers were bleeding him like they were bleeding everyone else in town, it wouldn't last long. Pretty soon, Mr. Gary wouldn't be any richer than the rest of them.

Sanders wondered what the Hawkins brothers would do then. Probably move on to some other town and take whatever they could get there, suck it dry like some kind of leeches, and then find somewhere else.

It never occurred to him that anything or anyone would put a stop to Sam and Ben Hawkins. No one had ever stood up to them before, not even the sheriff, and nobody ever would.

At least that's what Sanders thought.

Chapter Four

Sam Hawkins was sitting in a wooden frame chair with a leather bottom made from cowhide. The bottom was mostly worn smooth, but there were still tufts of reddish hair on the parts of the seat no one sat on.

The chair was on the porch of the house where Sam and Ben lived. It wasn't much of a porch, and it wasn't much of a house. The porch slanted forward just the littlest bit, and the roof leaked. It was no place to be when it rained. Inside the house wasn't that much better, but one could try to avoid the biggest leaks.

Ben was on the porch too, but he wasn't sitting in a chair. There wasn't another chair, and Sam was the older. He always got the chair. Ben sat with his back resting against the wall, his hat pulled down over his eyes. Above his head was a window with a broken pane.

The Hawkins brothers looked a great deal alike, but it was easy to tell them apart. Ben was the one who chewed tobacco. He was never without a plug in his pocket and a chaw in his cheek, bulging it out like he had a little round ball in there.

Both men had tangled black hair that had not been washed for some time and black beards that were in a similar condition. If a man looked close he could see the tobacco stains in Ben's beard, but no one wanted to look that close. Both men had the hooked noses that, along with their name, had given Sam his nickname.

They had wild black eyebrows, too, growing straight across their foreheads with no break above the nose. There were people who said that a bird could build a nest there and not be noticed, but they never said that to the Hawkins boys' faces.

Both Ben and Sam were wearing worn Levi's and faded plaid flannel shirts with long sleeves. The underarms of the shirts were stained with sweat. Their boots were scuffed and scarred, the heels worn down.

Sam was watching a terrapin crawl with infinite patience across the dirt yard.

"Where you think that son of a bitch is goin'?" he said.

Ben pushed up his hat and leaned forward. "What son of a bitch?"

"Out there in the yard," Sam said.

Ben squinted his eyes, trying to see whatever or whoever it was that Sam was talking about.

"I don't see nothin'," he said finally.

"It's a terrapin," Sam said. "Right over there." He pointed.

Ben looked again. "I see him," he said. He spit a stream of brown tobacco juice over the edge of the porch. "What about him?"

"I was just wonderin' where he thought he was goin'," Sam said.

"Hell," Ben said. "How should I know? What difference does it make, anyway?"

"Not a damn bit," Sam said. "He ain't ever gonna get there, anyhow."

Sam pulled a pistol from its holster, cocked it, and sighted down the barrel.

"You can't hit that thing from here," Ben said. He spit again. "I bet it's twenty yards off."

"I can hit it," Sam said. "Ten dollars says I can hit it."

Ben nodded. "Ten dollars says you can't."

Sam fired the pistol. The explosion was accompanied by grayish smoke, the smell of gunpowder, and a loud yowl from beneath the porch.

The bullet chipped off the top of the terrapin's shell and sailed up and away, whacking into the trunk of a pine tree.

The terrapin tumbled over and over, finally winding up on its back. It was apparently unharmed, and its legs waved slowly in the air as it tried to right itself.

"Missed," Ben said.

"Be damn if I did," Sam said. "Flipped the sucker four times."

A mangy-looking orange tomcat stalked out from under the porch and looked around. There were several patches where he had scratched out large hunks of his fur, as he was bothered considerably by fleas.

Ben and Sam were bothered by fleas, too, but they were not given much to scratching.

The cat did not see the terrapin. He sat down in the shade of the porch and began biting himself on the back.

Ben spit a thick brown stream of tobacco juice at the cat, which took no notice as the liquid spattered on the ground near him.

"Ten dollars," Ben said.

"That's right," Sam agreed. "You owe me ten."

"No, I don't. You owe *me* ten. You missed."

"I hit the bastard," Sam said. "You saw it."

"Didn't kill him, though," Ben said, leaning back against the wall and pulling down his hat.

"That wasn't the bet," Sam said. He was looking at the terrapin, which still hadn't managed to right itself. "You want to bet me ten more I can't kill him?"

Ben pushed up his hat, interested again. "Sure," he said. "Why not."

Sam fired again, and the pistol jumped in his hand. This time, the cat made no sound at all. It didn't even move.

The bullet hit the terrapin, which flew apart with a sharp cracking noise, as if someone had dropped it on a rock from a great height.

Fragments of the shell and bits of bloody flesh sailed through the air.

"Ten dollars," Sam said.

"I owe you," Ben said. "What're you gonna do about that terrapin?"

"Let the cat have him," Sam said.

The cat was already walking across the yard toward part of the remains. When he got there he sniffed them for a second then began to bite at something on one of the shell fragments. Sam and Ben did not feed him often. He had to take what he could find.

Sheriff Coy Wilson was sitting in the jail with his feet up on the desk, waiting out the heat of the day. He didn't like to go out on his daily patrol of the town until the heat moderated a little bit, which meant that it would be late afternoon before he did anything.

He was a short, fat man whose belly hung down over his gunbelt, and he didn't like to stir himself unless it was absolutely necessary. That's what he liked about working in this particular town—it was seldom necessary for him to stir. There were the usual number of saloon fights, and there was an occasional disagreement about the amount of a bill owed at one of the local stores. There might even be a fracas between a husband and a wife or between a couple of brothers, just family arguments that were easily settled. That was about all. It made the job of sheriffing pretty simple.

In fact, as far as the townspeople were concerned, it was complicated by only one other thing. The Hawkins brothers. They seemed to all appearances to have the town in their grip. They had just showed up one day a couple of years before and taken over.

They lived out there in the woods, and they did pretty much what they damn well pleased. If they rode into town and announced that all the merchants owed them twenty-five dollars, then the merchants paid up.

They didn't want to at first, but they did. They had learned about that the hard way, when old Tully Hairston, who had owned the general store at the time, refused to put in his ante.

The Hawkins boys didn't say anything to him about it. They just went on their way, collecting from all the others, and letting Tully think he'd called their bluff.

In fact, Tully had gone around to all the other stores that day, telling the owners what a big mistake they were making by paying off. He was a feisty little man, and he had really given everyone a tongue-lashing.

"You're just playin' right into their hands by givin' 'em what they ask for," he said. "You got to stand up to 'em, tell 'em you won't give them a damn cent. They won't do nothin' about it. We still got law in this town."

The others had tried to talk sense into Tully.

"Goddammit," Barclay Sanders told him. "You ought to know better than to talk like that. They won't let you get away with it. It's only twenty-five dollars, and they don't ask often. You should've given it to 'em, Tully. You're just gonna cause trouble for all of us."

"I don't think so," Tully said. "They're just like any other bullies. Cowards, the lot of 'em."

Baclay Sanders and the others didn't say anything else. They just shook their heads and let Tully go his own way.

That night, some visitors and there wasn't much doubt about who, rode into town and broke windows in front of Tully's store. They went inside and ripped open every bag, letting the contents run out on the floor. Flour, beans, coffee, sugar—the lot. Stomped around in it. Smashed the pickle barrel and the cracker barrel. Poured syrup over everything. Threw a wheel of cheese in the floor and mashed it all over. Shot the cans, splattering tomatoes and peaches around the walls.

Then they rode off.

The shooting had awakened a lot of folks, but by the time they got to the store, there was no one there.

Tully had complained to the sheriff, but that hadn't done any good. There was no proof that the Hawkins brothers had done a thing, and the sheriff refused to act without proof.

"Hell," he said. "That wouldn't be any more legal that what was done to that store. You can't just go accusin' folks of things because you *think* they did somethin'."

And that was that. Tully Hairston decided the hell with it and left town, went off to try ranching with his brother. He didn't even clean up the store. The rest of the merchants knew that Tully thought they were a bunch of spineless cowards, and maybe they were, but they still had their stores, and he didn't. Someone else opened the store again about a week later.

There wasn't much of a question about paying the Hawkinses after that, not that there had been much of one before. They came in when they needed the money, and they got it. They weren't greedy, but they took enough. People often wondered why they continued to live in that shack in the woods when they could have afforded better, but they sure weren't going to ask. They were afraid the Hawkinses might want to move to town. And if they did, there was no telling whose house they might take a shine to.

No one had bothered the Hawkins brothers after what happened at Tully's. The Reverend Stump, a few weeks before his marriage, had preached a hell/hot, heaven/high sermon about them, and everyone who heard it had secretly agreed with him.

The Hawkinses hadn't been in church, naturally enough, but they heard about the sermon. That night riders, and again it didn't take much imagination to figure out who, went over the preacher's picket fence, kicked through the flowers, threw horse manure all over his house, and shot out the stained-glass windows of the church.

They rode away just as the sheriff arrived, and once again he refused to go after the Hawkinses. There was no proof they were the guilty parties, though of course everyone in town knew that they were.

That was the last brave thing that the Reverend Stump did, unless you counted getting married.

No one really expected Sheriff Wilson to do anything. The town had hired him a few months before the Hawkins brothers appeared on the scene, and no one had told him he would have to confront anything like that. They had hired him for the kind of minor scrapes they were used to, and to tell the truth no one there thought they paid him enough to go up against anybody like those Hawkinses. They had never thought he'd have to.

He had drifted into town shortly after the natural death of old Sheriff Townsend, who had served for fifteen years and never faced anything worse than an angry drunk. Townsend had been nearly sixty when he had taken the job, and it had never strained him. No one thought Wilson would have to strain, either.

He seemed like an amiable enough fella, and he averred that he was able to use a gun and his fists, though he didn't like to and would prefer to avoid violence whenever possible.

It just wouldn't be possible when dealing with Sam and Ben, so the town didn't take it much amiss that he ignored them. There was occasional grumbling when the merchants got together, but no one really complained. Everyone was afraid that if they complained too much or too long, the sheriff would try to form a posse to go after the Hawkinses.

And there wasn't a one of them who was going to volunteer for that, for damn sure.

Carl Gary found the sheriff in the jail. Wilson didn't seem to think Gary was anything special. He didn't get up, didn't even swing his feet down off the desk.

Gary looked as if he might make something of that, but he decided better of it. Instead, he said, "Did you hear that there is a medicine show in town?"

"Is that a fact?" Wilson said. "Nope. I hadn't heard about it."

Gary was not surprised. Not only did Sheriff Wilson often fail to show the proper respect to the town's leading citizens, he was singularly uninformed about local events. Gary had been in favor of hiring Wilson for the job originally, but over the time Wilson had been in office, Gary had come to wonder if he and the rest of the town had not made a big mistake. The man was lazy and arrogant, and Gary did not like him.

"I thought you might not have heard," Gary said. "That's why I stopped by."

"That was mighty nice of you," Wilson said. He reached into his shirt pocket for a sack of tobacco and rolling papers. Without taking his feet off the desk, he deftly rolled a smoke and stuck it in his mouth. He opened a drawer of the desk and felt around in it for a second. His hand came out with a match, which he scratched on the underside of the desk. There was a popping sound and the hand came out holding the now-lighted match. Wilson applied the flame to the tip of his cigarette, inhaled, and blew out a cloud of smoke.

Gary stood there patiently watching the performance.

"Was there something else you had to say?" Wilson wondered.

"What are you going to do about it?" Gary said.

"'Bout what?"

"I expect there'll be trouble," Gary said.

Wilson inhaled again and blew a perfect smoke ring. "You said you *expected* trouble. That don't mean there'll be any. I can't act just on what people expect."

Gary moved a step closer to the desk. "See here, Sheriff. You know as well as I do what is bound to happen this evening, if the Hawkins brothers get wind of that medicine show being here. And they will get wind of it. They know everything that goes on in this town, unlike some people."

The sheriff shifted his weight and swung his feet off the desk. They hit the floor heavily.

"What's that supposed to mean?" he said, squinting through the haze of smoke that was forming between them.

"Nothing," Gary said. "But you know that they are going to demand payment from the show for allowing it to perform. That is, they are if they treat it like they treat everyone else in this community, and I see no reason why they should not."

"Well, now," Wilson said. "That may be so, or it may not. You can't go accusin' somebody of a crime they ain't even committed yet. That's worse than blamin' them for somethin' you ain't even sure they've done."

Gary tried not to let his disgust show. He was just a saloon keeper, but he tried to take an interest in the town, to make it a better place to live. That hadn't been easy to do since the Hawkins brothers showed up, and Wilson had not been much of a help.

"We know who does nearly everything that goes on around here," Gary said. "The crimes, too."

"Maybe you do," Wilson said. "Can't say as *I* do, though."

"You should," Gary said. Only a blind man could avoid seeing what's happening."

Wilson stood up. "Look," he said. "You don't have to pay any money to the Hawkins boys if you don't want to. I've never seen 'em force anybody to do it. I talked to 'em about it, and they said they were just askin' for contributions. Said they helped keep the town quiet, and people were grateful enough to give them a little money for doin' it."

"Keeping the town quiet is your job," Gary said. "We pay you to do that. We don't need the Hawkinses."

"Then don't pay 'em," Wilson said. "Simple as that."

"We've seen what happens to the people who don't pay," Gary said. "So have you."

"There've been a few little accidents, sure—"

Gary laughed. "Accidents? That's what you call what happened to Tully's store? To Stump's church? Accidents?"

"We never found who did it," Wilson said, shaking his head stubbornly. "There wasn't any evidence to say who was the guilty ones."

Gary was ready to give it up. Wilson's head was thicker than an oak log.

"All right, Sheriff," he said. "You're probably right. Those Hawkins brothers are pure as the driven snow, and Tully's store was probably savaged by a couple of stray dogs. I'm sorry if I've disturbed you."

He turned his back on the sheriff and walked out the door. He had done what he could. If the Hawkins brothers broke up the medicine show, that was too bad. He had tried to be a good citizen.

He thought for a moment of riding out and warning the operator of the show, but then decided that would be too much trouble. Let him take his chances like everyone else in town.

The sheriff watched Gary go. When the saloon owner was out the door, Wilson sat back down and put his feet up, taking one last puff on his cigarette before throwing it to the floor. He guessed he'd better take in the medicine show that evening, just to be sure things didn't get out of hand.

Chapter Five

It had happened three years ago, but Ray Storey would never forget a minute of it. He could still see it happening in his dreams, where it happened with agonizing slowness but where he was never able to stop it, any more than he had been able to stop it when it had happened in reality.

It was late in the afternoon, not long after the Fourth of July, and Ray and his brother, Chet, were walking down the boardwalk of the little Kansas town. Ray was holding a bag containing a pound of coffee, some dried pinto beans, and some canned goods. Chet was sucking on a peppermint that Ray had bought him.

Chet was six years younger than Ray, and he had never been quite like anyone else. He was a lovable kid, happy most of the time, always smiling, easily entertained, but he didn't have the kind of mind that took to book learning, or any kind of learning at all. The way the doctor had put it was that Chet would never really grow up.

Ray didn't mind taking care of his brother. He'd been doing it for quite a while now.

Their father had died in a fall from a horse when Chet was ten, and their mother had not lived for long after that. Some people thought that she had grieved herself to death, but Ray knew better. She hadn't been well, not even when her husband was alive. Whatever had killed her had been something that had eaten her away, all right, but it hadn't been grief. Her husband's death might have hastened the process, but she had been dwindling for years.

There had been a little money, not much, but enough so that Ray could keep the farm going. In a couple of years he was actually making a little money on his own.

And then there was the accident, if that was what you could call it.

It had been hot that day, and dusty. When he thought about it or dreamed about it, Ray could still feel the heat of the lowering sun on his back, still smell the dust of the street as it was kicked up by the hooves of the horses pulling a wagon going by, still hear the jangle of the harness.

They had been about a block from the bank when they heard the sound of shooting, the gun shots shattering the quiet air like rocks smashing through the smooth surface of a quiet pond.

Chet had started running, apparently thinking that the sounds were made by something he had been very impressed by only a few days before.

"Fireworks!" he yelled, the peppermint he still had in his mouth blurring the words. "Fireworks!"

Ray dropped the bag, the cans clattering on the boardwalk, beans scattering everywhere, and went after him.

Three men came running out of the bank. They were all wearing long dusters, and they were all heavily bearded, with hats pulled down low on their brows. Two of them were carrying canvas bags.

They were running for the horses that were tied to the hitch rail.

The whole town erupted in shooting at that moment. Someone from inside the bank fired at the retreating robbers, and they returned the fire.

The sheriff and one of his deputies came running from somewhere, guns roaring, and several men from nearby stores, realizing what was going on, ran outside and opened fire with rifles and shotguns.

In the middle of it all was Chet.

He was no longer yelling about fireworks. He had stopped in the middle of the street, a puzzled look on his face, his head twisting to the right and left as he looked for a way to run and escape the noise that crashed around him.

The three bank robbers were mounted now and returning fire both into the bank and at the townspeople as their horses reared and pitched. Then they charged down the street straight at Chet, who stood frozen in panic.

In his dreams since that day, Ray had made the run toward his brother a hundred times, two hundred, but it didn't matter. It always ended the same way.

It was as if his feet were mired in thick mud instead of running on the hard-packed, dusty street. He could hear the horses bearing down on him and Chet, almost feel their hot breath, and he could see his own hands again and again as he reached out to shove his brother out of the way.

He could see Chet turn his head slowly, slowly, and he could see Chet's eyes as they filled with fear and with the gradual realization of what was about to happen to him.

Then Ray would feel the heavy collision with the lead horse, feel his body being flung aside, feel the impact with the ground that drove the breath from him.

And he could hear Chet's scream as the horses ran him down.

Chet lived for ten long months after that, but Ray never saw him smile again.

It was hard to smile when you were paralyzed from the neck down, forced to spend what was left of your life motionless on a bed, never quite understanding what it was that was wrong with you. When your food probably tasted like dust and when you knew that you would never get out of that bed and walk again.

It was no surprise to Ray that Chet finally died, even though the town's doctor told Ray that there wasn't really anything wrong with the boy other than the paralysis.

"Tell you the truth," the doctor said, "he's about as healthy as anybody. Doesn't even have colds, much less fevers. But that doesn't necessarily mean he's all right."

"But he *is* all right," Ray said.

"Just some of him," the doctor said. "He'll never quite figure it all out, and what with him not being able to move so much as a finger, well, he just might get to wondering what it is that he has to live for. If he ever gets to that point. . . ."

The doctor didn't explain what would happen if Chet ever got to that point. He didn't have to. Ray got the idea.

He could almost have named the day when it happened. Chet had been trying to look out the window and see the snow that winter. He had always loved the snow, Ray knew, and they had always built a snowman in the front yard, putting an old coat and hat on it, with a couple of rocks for eyes and a corn cob for a nose.

Chet's eyes filled with tears as he watched the heavy flakes drift down, and Ray knew what he was thinking. He died not long afterward.

By then, Ray knew the name of one of the men who had robbed the bank.

"Sam Hawkins," the sheriff told him. "Not much doubt about it. Hard to tell under all that hair on his face, but that beard's one of Hawkins's trademarks. The teller recognized him from his wanted poster. It was Hawkins, all right."

"What about the men with him?" Ray said.

"Teller didn't get a good look at those two. One of 'em might've been Sam's brother, Ben. They run together, mostly. But can't anybody say for sure."

"The teller's positive about this Sam Hawkins, though?"

"You can ask him yourself."

"I think I might just do that. Do you have a copy of that poster you could let me have?"

44

The sheriff gave Ray the poster, which he took to the bank. The teller was certain that was the man.

"It's the eyes," the teller said. "You can tell by the eyes that he's a killer."

Ray kept the poster. He had already decided that if Chet died, someone was going to be sorry. The robbers had gotten away clean, along with over six thousand dollars of the bank's money in the canvas bags. They had ridden through the bullets and shotgun pellets and out of town, never to be seen again. Because of Chet as much as because of the money, the lawmen of several counties had joined in the hunt, but the three men had been too fast and too clever. Ray, however, was determined he would track them down sooner or later, or at least one of them, the one whose name he knew.

Sam Hawkins. A man whose regard for life was so low that he would run down a boy in the street, leaving him paralyzed for the rest of his short life. Or if he was not the man, he was one of them, and they were all equally guilty as far as Ray was concerned. He was resolved that Hawkins would pay.

He buried Chet in the back yard that winter, and when spring came he sold the farm.

Then he started hunting.

Ray Storey walked out of the saloon and took a deep breath of the East Texas air. Now that he appeared to have finally located Sam Hawkins, he felt strangely irresolute. He realized that the hunt had consumed so much of his life that he had not really made any plans about what he would do if he actually located the man.

At first it had seemed simple. He had even discussed it with the sheriff.

"You take him to the law when you catch up with him, if you ever do," the sheriff said. "That's what you got to do if you're really goin' to take off after him like this."

"I'm going after him," Storey said. "That's one thing for sure."

"Well, you don't want to go tryin' to be the law yourself. You don't have a badge, and that gun you're carryin' might not help you any if Sam Hawkins is as good as they say he is."

Ray had never carried a pistol before. He had bought it that winter right after Chet's death, and he had worn it ever since, every hour of the day, to get used to the feel of it. He hardly even noticed he had it on now, but he wasn't what you could call "good" with it.

"You know how to use that thing?" the sheriff said.

"I can use it," Ray told him, stretching the truth by a pretty good way. He could aim and shoot, but that was about all. He certainly was no marksman. The bullets didn't always go where he aimed them, no matter how much he practiced. Some people had a knack for shooting, but he didn't seem to be one of them.

"The secret's not to be the fastest," the sheriff said. "You just got to stand your ground and keep shootin'. That's what it takes: patience and not bein' afraid."

"I'm not afraid," Ray said, and he hadn't realized until today that he had been stretching the truth a little bit there, too. As he stood outside the Western Dandy, he knew that he was afraid, though he had not known it before.

It was probably that earlier, he had not been faced with the actuality of Sam Hawkins. Until now, the man had been nothing more than a name to him, a name that he associated with one particular hot afternoon. The man had been the cause of Chet's death, and Ray had promised himself that he wasn't going to let Hawkins get away with it, but promising was one thing. The reality was something else.

He looked down at the handbills he was clutching. He had almost forgotten the medicine show, which was, after all, his real reason for being in town. He told himself that he owed the Colonel the courtesy of doing his job and that he could not let his own desire for revenge ruin the show's appearance in the town. He would have to put off his visit to Sam Hawkins until it was time for the show to move on. Then he would tell the Colonel that he was leaving. The Colonel would protest, but he would just have to find himself a new Kit Carson. Ray Storey would be staying in town to settle the score with Sam Hawkins.

He conscientiously passed out the rest of the handbills, and then he headed back to where the show wagon was waiting.

"I would like for you to do a bit of trick shooting this evening to begin the show," the Colonel said. He and Ray were setting up the little raised platform beside the show wagon. The Squaw Ro-Shanna and Banju Ta-Ta required a slight elevation in order for the crowd to have the best view of them.

Ray started to protest. He did not like to do the trick shooting, which was actually trickier than any of the spectators realized, though not tricky in the way they might have conceived it. The Colonel or his wife would toss small, hollow clay balls into the air, and Ray would break them by shooting them with his pistols. He could generally break eight or nine of ten balls, but that was because he would be using shells loaded with birdshot instead of solid lead.

"Now remember," the Colonel said, brushing back his thick hair with one hand, "it's not really deception. It's merely a part of the show. Entertainment, my boy. That's what we're providing here. Entertainment. We're taking no bets on your abilities."

"All right," Ray said, giving in. He knew he wouldn't be doing it more than once or twice more before leaving the show, but he didn't tell the Colonel that. "I'll do it."

"Good. Good. A little shooting always starts us off with a bang." The Colonel smiled at his own joke. "Gets everyone in the mood for the rest of the show."

The Boozer staggered up at this point, having drunk his day's allotment. The Colonel never allowed him to drink within two hours of time for the show to begin.

"And a fine, mellow mood that will be," The Boozer declaimed. "I myself am looking far'ard to it." The last word was smothered in a discreet belch.

"Ah, Dr. Stuartson," the Colonel said. He never called him The

Boozer. "I was wondering if I might prevail upon you to do the anatomy lecture this evening."

"Wha-what's 'at? The lecture? Me?" Stuartson appeared dumfounded. So was Storey.

"Of course," the Colonel said. "And why not? Who better to expound on the mysteries of the human body than a man who has devoted the greater part—I may say, the better part—of his life to its study?"

"I—ah—I'm not sure. . . ."

"And why not? Why not use some of your expertise in a way that will be valuable to the show and give the customers something that they will appreciate and remember? What do you say, man?"

The Boozer tried to straighten himself, brushing at the sticks and dirt that clung to his wrinkled suit. "I—I could try. . . ."

"Fine, fine," the Colonel said, putting his hand on Storey's arm. "Come along, Ray. Let us allow Dr. Stuartson some time to get himself together and prepare his mind for the lecture that he will be giving. And a fine one it will be, I'm sure."

Though the Colonel's voice was generally a little louder than anyone else's he was pitching it to be sure that The Boozer overheard him.

"What was all that about?" Ray said when they had gotten some distance away.

The Colonel paused. "I think it might be time for our friend Dr. Stuartson to take a bit more responsibility in the day-to-day operation of the show."

"Why?" Ray said.

"To put it simply, I believe that he is capable of it," the Colonel said.

Ray shook his head, his long hair flopping around his neck. He didn't understand.

"My medicine can heal many things," the Colonel explained. "But it cannot heal Dr. Stuartson. He must heal himself, and I believe that he is now ready to do so."

The Boozer didn't look ready to Storey. He didn't look any different than he had for the past year, and Storey said as much.

"Not to you, perhaps," the Colonel said. "But you are not trained to see such things. I am."

Storey wasn't sure just what training the Colonel was referring to. From what Storey had gathered, the Colonel had never actually trained to do anything.

Nevertheless, Storey kept his mouth shut. He had seen some remarkable things happen since he had begun his association with the Colonel. He knew that the "medicine" they sold was nothing more than alcohol and water and a few other things, but he also knew that there were people who had come to the show looking frail and sickly and who had returned within twenty-four hours looking as healthy as pampered thoroughbreds, and they were generally singing the praises of the Colonel and his medicine.

Storey couldn't explain it, and neither could anyone else, though Storey was also aware of the Colonel's seeming belief in his own product and thought that belief, both the Colonel's and the customer's, might have something to do with it.

Storey had asked him about it once, but the Colonel had only smiled and said, "There are more things in heaven and earth than are dreamed of in your philosophy, my dear Kit Carson."

Storey wasn't even aware of having a philosophy, and when he mentioned that point the Colonel told him that he had been quoting from a play.

"Quite a famous one, too," he said, "and as entertaining as our own humble presentations, I must say. You should read it sometime."

He had pressed a copy of a well-thumbed collection of Shakespeare's plays on Storey, who had read *Hamlet* with a good deal of interest.

Somehow it had reminded him of his own situation, though he had always been sure that he would never put off his revenge the way the young Prince of Denmark had done.

That is, he had never thought so until today.

Chapter Six

Sheriff Coy Wilson sat on his horse and looked down at the Hawkins brothers, who were sitting on the porch of their shack in approximately the same positions they had been in all day. They didn't go in much for unnecessary movement.

The remains of the terrapin were still in the yard, only slightly chewed by the cat, which was back in the shade under the porch.

Ben Hawkins scratched his beard and spit into the dust near the forefoot of Wilson's horse.

"How you doin', Coy?" he said.

Wilson was not impressed with the accuracy of Ben's spitting or with anything else about him; he wasn't impressed with Sam either.

"Look at the two of you," he said, relaxing in the saddle, leaning forward a little and resting his belly on the pommel. "Sometimes I wonder why in the hell I ever hooked up with you in the first place."

Sam sat up a little straighter. "Just because you shaved off your beard and started wearin' a badge don't necessarily mean you're any better than us, Coy. You oughta try to remember that."

Wilson grimaced. "I remember it, all right. I'm just beginnin' to wish I didn't."

"I don't know as that I like the sound of that," Ben said. "What do you think, Sam? You think our pardner the sheriff is gettin' too big for his britches now that he's packin' a badge?"

Sam laughed unpleasantly. "He might be, at that. You'd think he never did anything wrong in his whole life, wouldn't you? Just look at him, sittin' there high and mighty on that bay horse, lookin' like he had himself a hot bath and a shave not more'n a day or so ago. Maybe he thinks he's a little bit better than his old friends. Maybe that's it."

Wilson's face was getting red as Sam spoke, but he kept his voice even. "I'm not thinkin' any such of a thing, and you better believe it. It was your idea, my takin' this law job when we rode up on this town, not mine."

"Sure has worked out for us, too, ain't it?" Ben said. "Old Sam, he's full of good ideas."

"Damn right I am," Sam said. He looked at Wilson. "If you hadn't run down that kid, we'd all be livin' high on the hog today instead of hangin' out around a whistle stop like this, tryin' to rob the people two bits at a time."

Wilson knew that Sam was right, in a way, but it hadn't really been his fault that he'd run the kid down. Hell, they were trying to get away from a bunch of angry citizens with guns and rifles. Who would've thought some damn kid would come running out into the street right in front of them? It was like the little bastard didn't have good sense.

"You can't get away with killin' a little kid," Sam said. "Folks don't like things like that. You take their money, they're gonna forget after a while. But you kill a kid, they think about it for a long time."

"I didn't kill him," Wilson said, knowing that it didn't really make much difference.

"Hell, you might as well have. Those damn laws kept after us for six months. I never thought I'd have to leave Kansas over a thing like that. You'd have thought it was their own money we took out of that bank."

"Yeah," Ben said. "And it don't look like we'll ever get to spend a dollar of it, the way things are goin'."

"We'll spend it," Wilson said. "Some day folks will forget about that kid. Besides, this is about the best hide-out we could've found, right out in the open like this. The Kansas lawmen don't get this far from home, and it won't be long before it'll be all right to go back to Kansas and enjoy that money. We'll have some more money by that time, too."

"Yeah," Sam agreed. "That's about the only thing that I like about this. We make a little money and have a little fun. I guess it ain't all bad."

"It ain't Kansas, though," Ben said, looking at the tall pines surrounding them. "I get tired of all these damn trees."

Sam nodded in agreement, but both the brothers knew that they had secretly enjoyed their stay in East Texas. They would never have admitted it to Wilson, but what they liked even better than the money they took in was their harassment of the townspeople. The money was all right, but for them it was just part of the game.

It was the same with the banks they had robbed in Kansas, for there had been more than one. The money was good, but what really mattered was the thrill of walking into a bank and showing the tellers and customers who was the boss. It was the looks on their faces when they saw the drawn pistols, the fear in their eyes as they were forced to lie on the floor, knowing that if they so much as looked up again they would probably never look at anything again.

Here, it wasn't quite the same, but it was just as good. If they were paid what they demanded, that was all right. But if they were refused, that was better. Then they could ride in, shoot out windows, trample yards, run roughshod over picket fences. And all with the cooperation and even the protection of the law.

In a way it was like shooting the terrapin. There was no reason for it, but it was fun to see it blasted apart.

"Yeah," Sam said finally. "Those trees do get worrisome after a while. When you reckon we can leave this place, Coy?"

That was a topic that Wilson had given considerable thought to lately. He had a plan.

"I been thinking about that," he said, looking around at the trees, listening to the faint breeze stirring in the pine needles and smelling the freshness of the trees. He liked the place, himself, and he wondered why he hadn't come there long ago. The thought of heading back to the treeless plains of Kansas had absolutely no appeal for him. His plan was to stay in Texas and let the brothers go back without him. He would be glad to be free of them.

"Hard to believe you actually been thinkin'," Sam said. "You gonna tell us what you've come up with, or are we supposed to guess?"

"I'll tell you. I figure that you two have taken in about all you can around here, except for one little bit, and I'll tell you about that in a minute. Anyhow, I think it's time that I started to take my job serious and ran you off."

Ben stood up slowly, stretched, and spit. "Run us off? Did I hear you right, Coy? You say you were gonna run us off?"

Wilson shifted his weight in the saddle, and the horse snorted nervously.

"I didn't mean that like you took it, Ben," Wilson said.

"How did you mean it, then?" Sam said. He too had stood up. His head nearly touched the roof of the porch.

"I meant that's what it would look like had happened. I'd tell folks that I'd finally had enough of you and ride out here. Then I'd ride back and tell 'em that I'd run you off. That they wouldn't have to be worried about you anymore."

"And what is it that's gonna get you fed up like that?" Ben said.

"That's the other part of what I was gonna tell you," Wilson said. "You see, there's a medicine show in town. . . ."

The crowd began to gather early. There wasn't a great deal of excitement in the small town, and the medicine show was a welcome spectacle.

There were mostly men, but a few women mixed in. Most of them would pretend to be scandalized by the Squaw Ro-Shanna's talk, if they stayed for it, and they might not even have to pretend about Banju Ta-Ta's dance. They would certainly all be gone before the anatomy lecture if things went along as they usually did.

Or at least so The Boozer devoutly hoped. He was beginning to wonder just what he had let himself in for, and his throat burned as if he had been walking in the desert for a week without a sip of water.

He desperately needed a drink, and not of water, either, but there was nothing available. The Colonel kept the supply under strict control, and there was nothing for The Boozer to do but sit in the tent, sweat, and stare at his trembling hands.

Outside, the Colonel was getting the crowd in the right mood for the show.

"I know that many of you have already met Mr. Kit Carson in town earlier today," he said, waving his hand in the direction of Ray Storey, who was standing modestly to one side, still wearing his fringed buckskins. There was a murmur of agreement from the crowd.

"And no doubt many of you have heard of Mr. Carson's legendary ability with a six-gun," the Colonel went on.

"Kit Carson's, mebbe," someone called out from the crowd. "But not this here fella's."

There was laughter at the remark, but the Colonel was not perturbed. He had half expected both the comment and the laugh; it certainly wasn't the first time that the authenticity of Kit Carson had come into question.

"Well, now," the Colonel said. He was standing on the little platform that he and Storey had erected, with the red, white, and blue medicine wagon as his backdrop. He was wearing a top hat and a cut-away coat, a white shirt and flowing tie. "It appears that one of you harbors some doubts as to Mr. Carson's mastery of his weapon. I propose to offer you a small sample of his abilities at this time."

"How much you gonna charge us?" a voice said, to the accompaniment of more laughter.

The Colonel smiled tolerantly. "Not one penny, my friends. This little exhibition is absolutely free. Are you ready, Mr. Carson?"

Ray walked to the front of the platform. "I'd like for you all to step back a little and give me some room," he said.

The crowd moved back, clearing a space of about six feet in front of the platform.

"Ladies and gentlemen," the Colonel intoned, "may I present the Squaw Ro-Shanna!"

His wife emerged from the back of the wagon to the muffled sound of an Indian tom-tom being beaten somewhere inside and walked to the platform. At that moment, not a single person in the crowd was looking at Ray Storey. All eyes were on Ro-Shanna in her "authentic" Indian garb, which consisted of a very short buckskin skirt fitted with silver medallions around its hem and fringed like Ray's Kit Carson outfit. But it was the beaded buckskin shirt that attracted the most attention, and not for its beads. It was cut quite low, and it was very tight. The buttons seemed to strain to contain the Squaw Ro-Shanna's ample breasts, whose rounded tops were fully exposed to view. The men were torn, not knowing whether to look first at her breasts or at her ankles.

As they strained their eyes, they grew very quiet, almost holding their breaths. The outraged women hissed at their husbands, jabbing them in the ribs with sharp elbows or pulling at their arms to urge them to leave.

One of the men felt the sweat pop out on the top of his bald head as his face suddenly reddened. The Reverend Lawton Stump had not expected to see a sight such as this, and it shamed him to realize that his sinful human nature was excited by it. He knew that some of his parishioners had already noticed him there and that he would hear about it later, but he could not stop himself from looking.

On the other side of the crowd, carefully concealing herself among the others there, Naomi Stump was not looking at her husband. She too was watching Ro-Shanna, but she was not thinking so much about how the woman looked; she was wondering what effect a woman like that would have on Mr. Kit Carson. And she was wondering how she herself, dressed in the same outfit, would compare to Ro-Shanna. She thought the comparison would be a favorable one, for though the woman on the platform was quite attractive, she was obviously some years older than Naomi was.

Ro-Shanna was carrying a small cloth bag that she now handed to the Colonel. Storey's hands had started to sweat. He hoped he wouldn't make too much of a fool out of himself.

The Colonel reached into the bag and took out one of the hollow clay balls, proclaiming, "And now, ladies and gentlemen, Mr. Kit Carson!"

He threw the ball into the air without warning as he spoke, and Storey's hand flashed for his pistol. While he had never become extremely accurate, he had developed a facility for the fast draw that was quite effective in performance. He had never been forced to test it under any other conditions.

The gun cleared leather smoothly, and when the shot blasted the still air, there was a sharp intake of breath.

The ball shattered into five or six pieces above the heads of the crowd, the breath was released, and there was scattered laughter and applause.

Ray Storey began to relax a little. He always felt better after the show had actually started, and hitting the first one was a good sign.

The Colonel tossed up another ball, a bit higher this time, and Ray hit that one, too. Then both the Colonel and Ro-Shanna threw balls. This part was always tricky, but they had practiced throwing so that the balls were fairly close together, though not so close that they would be shattered by the same shot. The idea was for Ray to be able to trigger off two shots very rapidly without really having to move the muzzle of his gun a great distance. When it worked, it was quite effective, and it worked this time.

Two shots rang out, both balls splintered apart, and the crowd applauded enthusiastically.

Naomi Stump thought that Kit Carson was quite probably the

most wonderful man she had ever seen. He would know how to take a woman into his muscular arms and crush her to him, not treat her like some porcelain doll the way her husband did.

Her husband, on the other side of the crowd, was not really interested in the shooting exhibition. He was still focused on Ro-Shanna, and he pulled a spotless white handkerchief from inside his coat and patted the top of his head.

Ray shot five times, not missing a single time. It was a good beginning for the show, and the Colonel decided not to press his luck by any more shooting.

"A remarkable demonstration, Mr. Carson," he said, bringing the exhibition to an end, "and we thank you heartily for it. As you can see, ladies and gentlemen, the competence of Mr. Kit Carson has not been exaggerated, no matter what stories you might have heard of his exploits with a six-gun."

"What about that there big knife he carries?" a heavy-set man with a ragged vest said.

"Ah, the knife is another story, to be told at another time," the Colonel said. To avoid being questioned further, he turned to his wife. "Let me introduce to you once again the Squaw Ro-Shanna."

Mrs. Mahaffey smiled and bowed demurely, but not so demurely as to avoid showing a bit of cleavage. There was robust applause from all the men.

"This wonderful and wise woman," the Colonel said, "has assisted me in the development of one of the most potent medicines known to modern man, the incomparable Indian Vitality Pills. She has a story to tell you that will, quite literally, I think, change many of your lives for the better. It will remove forever the pain of every man's—" the Colonel's voice dropped to a near whisper, though it still carried far beyond the edge of the crowd "—Secret Sorrow."

It was very quiet now, and Ray Storey heard a bird call back in the trees.

"But first," the Colonel said, his voice assuming its usual robust tones, "I want to tell you about Indian Miracle Oil. Do any of you have wounds or sores that are slow to heal? Indian Miracle Oil, applied directly to the skin, speeds the healing process. Do you suffer from irritated kidneys? Stomach wind? Taken internally, Indian Miracle Oil will effect an almost instant cure! Do you have a cow or a sheep suffering from the bloat? Indian Miracle Oil is good for man or beast!"

The pitch went on, the Colonel's voice having an almost hypnotic effect except on those who were most used to hearing his pitch. Ray Storey looked out over the crowd to see who was there. His eyes almost instantly met those of Naomi Stump, who blushed and lowered her own gaze modestly. He remembered her from the dry goods store.

There could be trouble there, he knew. It would not be the first time that a woman had found herself attracted to him, and he had no interest in seeking entertainment with any woman of the town. That was one of the first lessons the Colonel had given him.

"A man can't be too careful," the Colonel had said. "Some of these women, they have no excitement in their lives, and they might see one of us as a way to find some. To them, we might appear to have a freedom and a romance about us that their lives do not provide. They are mistaken, of course, but you must never allow yourself to become involved. Especially should the woman be married. The complications are too hazardous to contemplate."

Storey let his eyes wander on.

"But," the Colonel was saying to the crowd, "even Indian Miracle Oil is not efficacious merely on its own. It must never be administered by one who has not beheld the Indian Healing Dance. Let me repeat that and caution you: Never let someone else have your bottle of Miracle Oil. Never lend it to a friend who has not witnessed the sacred dance. Never! I cannot be responsible for the consequences if you do!"

"All right, then, how's about the dance," yelled a squint-eyed man with a gray beard. "I'd sure like to see that there squaw do one!"

The Colonel drew himself up. "The Squaw Ro-Shanna does not perform the sacred Healing Dance. It is not of her tribe. But we have one associated with us who has been initiated into the secrets of the dance, one who can perform it for you right here on this platform."

From inside the wagon the low beating of the tom-tom which had accompanied Ro-Shanna's entrance could be heard again.

"Well bring her on, then!" a voice cried.

"First I must ask you one thing," the Colonel said. "I must ask you never to reveal what you have seen here tonight. The Indian Healing Dance is a secret of one of the great tribes, and Banju Ta-Ta, the Indian maid, has vowed never to dance again if her secret is uncovered to any except those who view her here on this platform."

"We know how to keep our mouths shut," a bearded man near the front said. "Let's get on with it."

"Very well then," the Colonel said. "May I present the Indian maiden! Banju Ta-Ta!"

By the time Louisa Mahaffey had gotten to the platform, writhing sinuously to the beat of the small tom-tom she carried in the crook of her left arm and beat with the fingers of her right hand, it was safe to say that most of the men in the crowd were no longer looking at her mother.

Her skirt was much longer than the one Ro-Shanna was wearing, but as Banju Ta-Ta swirled and spun onto the platform, the dress billowed out and up, exposing her trim calves, even affording a glimpse of her firm thighs.

There were audible gasps from the women in attendance, several of whom stalked away with an explosive "Well, I never!" or "Brazen hussy!"

Their husbands continued to watch avidly, particularly the Reverend Stump, whose handkerchief was now quite soaked with perspiration from having passed numerous times over the top of his head.

Banju Ta-Ta, however, had eyes only for one man, Ray Storey, who stood uncomfortably off to one side and tried to pretend that he did not know where the heat of her gaze was directed.

His daughter's looks were not lost on the Colonel, who had been trying to tell himself for some time that there was nothing in them.

He knew now that he was lying to himself. Louisa was fiercely interested in young Mr. Storey, no doubt about it. The Colonel hoped that no trouble would come of it. Storey had joined their little troupe and fit in quite well and done his job without undue complaint, but he had never confided in the Colonel his reasons for joining them, reasons which the Colonel had often wondered about. He knew that it went beyond the desire for money or the travel that the show provided.

It was not the Colonel's business to question his employees about such things, as a general rule, but it was becoming apparent that he was soon going to have a right to do so. He would have felt somewhat better about matters if Storey had shown a greater interest in Louisa, but it often seemed that Storey was preoccupied with matters he preferred not to discuss with anyone.

Banju Ta-Ta continued to twirl and beat the tom-tom, slowly increasing the tempo until it seemed that she might fly into the air. The Colonel and his wife had unobtrusively moved off the stage so that their daughter could have the entire space to herself.

There was not a man present whose blood was not stirred by the dance, not a one of them who was not ready—in fact, more than ready—to buy at least one bottle of Indian Miracle Oil.

But there were two others present who were not at all interested in buying. True, they were not at the platform, but their interests lay in other things.

"She ain't bad lookin' for an Injun, is she?" Ben Hawkins said, spitting accurately between his horse's ears and onto the trunk of a tree three feet away.

"Don't look bad from here, that's for sure," Sam said.

"What say we ride in an take over?" Ben said.

Sam looked at his brother with mild disgust. Sometimes Ben could be exasperating.

"Not yet," he said. "We do it like Coy said. We wait till they've sold their stuff, then we ride in. We don't want to have to rob ever' man there. If we wait, the money's all in one place and we just take it."

Ben didn't say anything. He didn't like waiting.

But he sure did like watching the dance.

"You reckon there'll be a lot of money?" he said after a second or two.

"It won't really matter," Sam told him. "It's just a way to make Coy look better when he runs us off, and it oughta be easy pickin's."

"I wouldn't mind pickin' up on somethin' besides the money," Ben said, his hot eyes still on Banju Ta-Ta.

"Coy wouldn't like that a damn bit," Sam said.

"Yeah," Ben agreed. "But Coy don't run me."

Sam just shook his head. Ben was contrary sometimes. It was best just to let him have his way. If he wanted to cause a little extra trouble, what would it hurt? Coy wanted people mad, didn't he? It looked like he was going to get what he wanted.

Chapter Seven

After the dance was completed, Banju Ta-Ta returned to the back of the wagon to great applause. The enthusiastic men were practically panting to buy a bottle of Indian Miracle Oil, but the Colonel was not yet ready to bring it out. There was more to the show than the dance, after all.

Banju Ta-Ta retreated to the interior of the wagon, and her father gave things a few minutes to cool down, using the silence to tell the crowd a few more things about the wonders of his healing concoction.

Most of the women had left by now, one or two even having been successful in dragging their husbands along, and the few who were left, with the exception of Naomi Stump, were plainly uncomfortable at being there. With the women leaving and the men still thinking about the dance, hardly anyone seemed interested in what the Colonel had to say, but at least they were respectfully silent.

The sun was beginning to sink, and shadows from the nearby trees played over the ground. The air was cooler, and the sky was beginning to take on a reddish hue near the horizon when the Colonel finished talking and deemed that the time was right for the festivities. He called for Banju Ta-Ta to bring out his banjo.

He managed a couple of passable tunes, his enthusiasm as he strummed covering up most of the missed fingerings, but the crowd was clearly more interested in Ro-Shanna. After a few choruses of "Sweet Betsy from Pike," the Colonel called her over.

Ro-Shanna took the stage and raised her face and arms heavenward in supplication. Her eyes were closed. Then she lowered her head and looked at the crowd.

"Once," she said, "my tribe was as numerous as the buffalo, as numerous as the flying birds. Every year more and more beautiful babies were born to gladden the hearts of their mothers and swell the pride of their fathers."

She smiled to express the joy the tribe felt, but after a moment her face turned solemn.

"That time of happiness lasted for many moons, and then it came to an end. No one knew why. It was as if bad medicine had been made for our people by some unknown enemy. Fewer and fewer babies were born each year, until one year there were only three. Then two. Then one."

Her eyes were now hollow with sorrow, her voice husky. The Colonel and Ray Storey stood to the side, watching her deferentially.

Ro-Shanna described an arc with her arms. "The world was filled with sadness for my people then. No longer did the sun light up the sky, no longer did the birds sing."

There was a lengthy pause as Ro-Shanna stared at the platform beneath her feet. Then she spoke again, her head still lowered. "No longer did the children play at the feet of their mothers. No longer did their grandparents hug them to their breasts for comfort."

The Colonel stepped over beside her and lifted up her head with a gentle hand. "And can you tell us why this came about, Ro-Shanna?"

She looked at his bright eyes. "The Secret Sorrow of our men," she said.

"And was there no cure, no way to make the babies play again?"

"We thought it not to be so," Ro-Shanna said. "But we were wrong. One day a man arrived in our camp, a man of our own tribe who had long ago left to travel over the world in search of knowledge. He had come back to us at last from the far mountains."

She stared out over the heads of the crowd, as if she were seeing into a distance they could not comprehend and seeing the far mountains themselves. The Colonel felt his own breast swell with pride. What an actress she was!

"In the mountains, the man had seen a strange sight. Something that for a long time he could not understand."

"And what was that strange sight, Ro-Shanna?" the Colonel said.

"Rabbits," she said. "Rabbits everywhere. Small ones, large ones, male and female."

The Colonel was surprised and taken aback. "But there are no rabbits in the mountains!" he said.

"So we thought too, but the man swore to us that he had seen them. More than he could count. They covered the sides of the hills as the stars that cover the night skies."

"But how could that be?"

"He watched the rabbits for a long time," Ro-Shanna said. "And after much study he realized that the rabbits were all eating an unusual and wonderful plant that grew in those mountains and that grew nowhere else. The rabbits fed on that plant, and they lived where no rabbits should have been living. They not only lived but they thrived. They not only thrived, but they increased their tribe almost daily. The man could not count the number of tiny rabbits being born."

"And it was the plant that caused all this?" the Colonel said, expressing the curiosity that by now filled the speechless crowd. "It was the plant that spurred the miracle of the births?"

"It was the plant," Ro-Shanna acknowledged. "He had brought some of it with him, and with the help of our medicine man he taught us how to boil it and make it into a pill which our men could eat."

The Colonel appeared to be hanging on every word, as if he had never heard the story before. As if he had not written it all down himself for his wife to memorize.

"What happened when they ate?"

Ro-Shanna's face beamed. "Our men were made new. The Secret Sorrows were no more! And the next year there were babies once again, more babies than ever before! Our tribe increased daily, and the men were proud again!"

The crowd was murmuring now. The men were getting really interested in the story with its obvious message about the efficacy of the Indian Vitality Pills that the Colonel's handbill advertised. Now they wanted to hear more.

"And those pills, Ro-Shanna?" the Colonel said. "Could you duplicate them again?"

"I made a pledge to my father, a medicine man who helped to make the first pills, that I would devote my life to helping others. What better way of helping than by sharing the secret of vitality?"

"But the strange plant? Are you able to obtain it?"

"I have traveled myself to the far mountains," Ro-Shanna said with becoming humility. "I have seen the plant, and I have picked it with my own hands. I have made the pills, and I have brought them here."

At her last words, the Colonel began to applaud loudly, and soon the rest of the crowd was applauding with him.

"I sure do wish we coulda heard what she was talkin' about," Ben Hawkins said. He was leaning forward in his saddle as if he could get close enough to hear by doing so. "Listen to all that clappin'."

Sometimes Sam wondered just how dumb his brother really was. "It was the turtle story," he said. "They all have a story like that. A man'd think you'd never been to a medicine show, to hear you talk."

Ben appeared genuinely puzzled. "The turtle story?"

"Hell, turtles, doves, buffaloes, it don't make any difference. Some kind of animal that lives off somewhere and has a lot of babies. Didn't you look at the handbill Coy showed us and see about the Vitality Pills?"

"I looked at it. I didn't see any damn turtles, or birds and buffaloes, either." Reading was not one of Ben's strong points.

"Never mind," Sam said. He wasn't going to waste his breath explaining things to Ben, who had heard the story about the turtles at the same medicine show Sam had. If he didn't remember, that was just too damn bad.

"I wish they'd quit all the talkin'," Ben said. "Why don't they get around to the sellin'?"

"Don't worry," Sam said. "They will."

"She's a damn good-lookin' woman, ain't she?" Ben said, his eyes on Ro-Shanna. "I still think we oughta take her with us. It's been a while since I had a woman like that."

It had been more than a while, Sam thought. Ben had never had a woman like that, and neither had Sam.

"We'll see," Sam said. Hell, even if it was Ben's idea, it wasn't a bad one.

Unaware of the watchers in the trees, the Colonel was getting ready to do his selling. He had finished telling the admiring crowd what a great humanitarian gesture the Squaw Ro-Shanna was making by offering them the Indian Vitality Pills, and now he was getting down to the good part.

"And, my friends, I have even better news for you all. I have personally been so inspired by Ro-Shanna's story that I am not going to sell you the Indian Vitality Pills."

There was an immediate outbreak of muttering among the crowd.

"What the hell you mean, you ain't gonna sell 'em?" the bearded man near the front yelled. "If you got 'em, we're gonna buy 'em. You got no right not to sell 'em to us."

Ray Storey had to turn away to hide a smile as the Colonel raised a palm to quiet things down. Storey had seen the Colonel use the same tactic hundred times in the past year, but it never failed to work.

"No, no, my friends," the Colonel said. "You misunderstand me. I did say that I would not sell you the pills, but what I meant was not what you think. I meant to say that I was going to *give* them to you absolutely free, though their value, as clearly printed on my handbills, is three full dollars!"

"Free?" the bearded man said. "You mean you're just gonna give 'em to us right here and now?"

"Right here and now," the Colonel said. "Please, Ro-Shanna. Mr. Carson."

Storey and Ro-Shanna went to the back of the wagon, where Louisa handed them boxes of Indian Miracle Oil and tins of pills. Then she joined them with a box of her own. They walked to the platform.

The Colonel beamed at them as they took their places beside him. "Of course," he said, "my friends and I have to make a living. We do have something to sell, the magic elixir known as Indian Miracle Oil, which relieves catarrh when taken in moderate doses, eases the bite of fleas when applied to the skin, and alleviates the symptoms of dropsy. And all for the price of only one dollar!"

"Yeah," someone yelled, "but what about them pills you was gonna give us?"

"I said that I would give them to you, and that is exactly what I intend to do. This afternoon, with every purchase of Indian Miracle Oil, you will receive absolutely free a tin of Indian Vitality Pills! Let me repeat that. Although the value of these pills is three dollars, they are yours free with the purchase of Indian Miracle Oil at the usual price of only one dollar. You heard that correctly, gentlemen! Only one dollar! Now who will be the first to buy?"

Hands holding money went up all over the crowd as everyone vied to be first.

"Me, me! I'll be the first!"

"Over here! Hey, over here! I've got a dollar!"

Storey, Ro-Shanna, and Banju Ta-Ta walked through the crowd, dispensing bottles and tins and taking in the money. It was not long before Banju Ta-Ta gave the famous medicine show cry.

"All sold out, Colonel!" she said. She held her empty box above her head.

Storey was not surprised that she had been the first to sell all her wares. For some reason, no matter how eager the men were to buy, it seemed that they still tried to buy from her. He took a dollar from a man in a dirty vest and handed him his pills.

"All sold out, Colonel!" Ro-Shanna said.

Again it was no surprise. At nine shows out of ten both women sold out before Storey. He still had a few bottles left, but men who had not been able to get to the women were crowding around him and his supply would soon be gone.

As he took in another dollar, he noticed that there was a woman standing near him. Now that was a surprise. He did not recall having sold a woman anything in the whole time he had been with the show. It was the woman who had been looking at him earlier.

Naomi Stump was slightly ashamed of what she was about to do, but she was determined to carry it through. She clutched her dollar in her warm, damp hand and edged closer to Storey. She thought again what a strong man he must be, and how unfavorably her stout, bald husband compared to him. If only the pills could transform Lawton into someone like Kit Carson! She did not think it was really possible, but she was certainly not going to let the chance pass her by.

"Please," she said. "I'd like a bottle of the Miracle Oil."

The men standing by them looked at her oddly, but Storey didn't mind. "Do you want the pills, too?" he said.

"Please." She handed him the dollar, and he gave her the last bottle and tin.

"All sold out, Colonel!" he said. He started toward the platform where the Colonel and the two women were waiting for him to join them.

From where they were watching in the trees, Ben Hawkins said, "Now, Sam?"

Sam nodded. "Now," he said.

The Reverend Lawton Stump was horrified to see that his very own wife was in the press of men around Kit Carson. Could she possibly be purchasing one of the heathen cures offered by the putative Colonel on the platform? It was bad enough that his own desires had been inflamed by the dance and then by the story told by the woman in the revealing shirt.

On the other hand, he told himself, he should not have been surprised. Naomi was not as conventional a wife as was it truly becoming for a minister to have, and she was likely to do anything that came into her head. That was another of the qualities that had attracted him to her in the first place, before he realized his folly. He wondered if she would try to slip the pills into his food and further contribute to the sinfulness of his flesh. He would have to be on his guard.

He had thought when he came to the show that he would buy the pills himself, as an aid to overcoming the feelings of guilt he told himself were both irrational and harmful, but he had not been able to go through with the purchase.

Now all he wanted to do was slip quietly away before anyone got the idea that he had actually gone through with buying anything. His reputation was probably damaged beyond repair already with those who had seen him at the show, though he might be able to convince most of his members that he had been there merely to observe and look into the moral qualities of the show. But Naomi's presence there was sure to be the talk of the town tomorrow.

He began edging toward the trees, thinking that he would slink behind the tent near the wagon and take a circuitous route to town, and so he was the first to see the two men charging out of the woods.

They seemed to be heading straight for the tent, and Stump opened his mouth to yell. Then he saw their drawn pistols, and the yell stuck in his throat.

In the tent, The Boozer heard the horses' hooves striking the hard ground and he wondered what was going on. He had been staring at the poster of the divided woman, halfway listening to the goings on outside, and he knew that it was not yet quite time for the anatomy lecture that always concluded the show.

He thought that it might be a good idea to look outside.

The Colonel was telling everyone that there would be one more show, to be presented the following evening, when more Indian Miracle Oil and Vitality Pills would be available. He urged everyone to try out his restorants before returning to tell others about them.

"But before you find your way home," he said, "I would like to invite you to attend an informative illustrated lecture on human anatomy, conducted by the estimable Albert Stuartson, M.D., in the tent just to your right. Due to the delicacy of the subject, women and children are of course not admitted."

Everyone turned to look at the tent. Dusk was gathering now, and the tent was glowing softly with the lantern that The Boozer had lit inside it earlier. No one was really interested in how the tent looked in the twilight, however. They were all very curious about what was inside.

That is, they were all curious until they saw the two mounted men riding toward them, pistols waving in the air.

Sam and Ben, knowing that they now had everyone's full attention, began firing their pistols into the crowd. Flame and smoke leapt from the pistol muzzles as the brothers guided their horses right by the tent, and each fired a shot into the canvas, leaving a black-rimmed hole. Then they continued firing into the crowd.

The Boozer, frightened nearly witless, but nevertheless thankful to have gotten out when he did, stumbled to the back of the show wagon and fell inside. At the moment, he did not care a whit what the Colonel's rules were. He was going to find something to drink.

The crowd was scattering, people running in all directions. Two men fell to the ground as they were struck by bullets. Others leaped into their buggies or climbed as fast as they could onto the backs of their horses and made tracks for town.

Ray Storey stared at the bearded men bearing down on the platform. He knew it was the Hawkins brothers, beyond a doubt, and he had a terrible feeling that he was watching something that had already happened to him once before.

This time, he had to do something about it.

He tried to force himself to draw his pistol, but for some reason his hand would not move. A sudden cold sweat popped out all over his body.

And then he saw the woman.

Naomi Stump was right in the path of the horses. She too seemed unable to move, and she simply stood there, one hand pressed to her mouth, watching as the horses thundered toward her.

Just as the Hawkins brothers got to Naomi, their horses veered apart, and they galloped past her, leaving her untouched. Then she moved, but only to collapse to the ground in a faint.

Sam and Ben reined their horses to a stop in front of the platform where the Colonel stood with his wife and daughter. Storey stood beside them, close enough to Sam and Ben to feel the hot breath of the horses on his face. Yet he still could not draw his pistol.

Most of the crowd had disappeared now, their horses' hoofbeats no longer even an echo in the clearing. They knew what was going to happen, and they wanted no part of it. Their own homes and businesses had suffered enough from the depredations of the Hawkinses, and no one wanted to get involved in this new fight and let himself in for more of the same.

Sam and Ben's horses pawed and snorted while the two riders looked disdainfully at the Colonel and the others, and just for fun Sam fired a shot into the boards of the platform right at the Colonel's feet.

The Colonel did not flinch. He might not have been a real colonel, but he knew how to act the part in times of danger.

"What is the meaning of this?" he said.

Sam and Ben laughed, their mouths hardly showing in their beards.

"What is the meaning of this?" Sam mocked. "The meaning of this is, you've got some money, and we want it."

"Yeah," Ben said. "So give it to us." he spit into the dust and leered at Banju Ta-Ta. "And them women ain't so bad, either. I may take me one of them with me, too."

"Oh, no, you won't," the Colonel said. There was something in the tone of his voice, a strength and authority, that Ray Storey admired tremendously. It might have been acting, but it sounded real enough.

Ben was impressed, too. "To hell with that, anyway. Give us the money." He spit tobacco juice again, splashing it on the platform. This time, the Colonel moved his foot.

"Go ahead and give them the money," the Colonel said, as if it didn't matter much to him one way or the other.

Storey and the women did as he said, handing the money to Sam, who put it in a cloth bag he had stuffed inside his shirt.

"Well, now, that was pretty easy," Sam said. "Kinda like stealin' from a little kid." Looking around, he saw the two fallen men. "Wonder how those fellas would feel about knowin' how you gave in so sweet-like?"

To tell the truth, Sam was disappointed. He actually liked for his victims to fight back. It added a little spice to things.

He glanced contemptuously at Storey. "I'd have thought a big fella like you would at least have put up *some* kind of a fight."

Storey said nothing. There was nothing he could say. He burned with fury inside, but outwardly he was stone. It was a if the cords of muscle inside his gun arm had been cut and he could not will them to move.

"What about that woman over there?" Ben said, noticing that Naomi was still lying in the dirt.

"What woman?" Sam said.

"That one over there," Ben said. "The one that fell out when we rode by her. She was a pretty little piece, looked like to me. And she weren't no injun, either."

He spit in the direction of Banju Ta-Ta, who looked as if she would like to spring on him, drag him from the saddle and rip his throat out with her bare hands. The Colonel put a restraining hand on her arm.

"Hell, take the one that's passed out, then." Sam said. He didn't care. They would be leaving this place soon, and it didn't much matter what they did. If they took the woman, that might just make Coy look like even more of a hero when he supposedly ran them off.

Ben rode over to Naomi, and while Sam kept the others covered he got down and lifted Naomi onto his horse like a sack of grain. Then he climbed back into the saddle.

"Looks like it's gonna be a good night tonight," he said.

"Yeah," Sam said. "I guess it is. Let's go."

He wheeled his horse, fired a shot over his shoulder, and the brothers rode away, their horses kicking up clods of dirt and clouds of dust in the fading light.

Chapter Eight

The Reverend Lawton Stump watched in horror as the two men nearly allowed their horses to trample his wife, but he watched in safety, having slipped behind the tent where he could not be seen.

He felt that he should go to her aid when she fell, though he was able to convince himself that there was nothing he could do. He was not armed, after all, and two men on horseback certainly looked like killers to him. What if they shot him? What good would he be able to do anyone then? Perhaps his wife was unharmed. He could go to her when the men got what they wanted and left.

But when he saw the man picking up his wife and putting her on the horse, he felt a jolt of pure revulsion. What must they be planning to do with her?

It was an easy question to answer, and he knew that the moment had come for him to step from behind the tent and declare his presence, at the same time demanding that the two men put down his wife and leave her with her lawful husband.

The moment had come quickly, and it passed with equal swiftness while Stump did absolutely nothing. Nothing, that is, except to stand exactly where he was and watch the two men ride away.

When he was sure they were gone, he slipped away into the darkness and began the walk toward town.

Ray Storey's face was burning. He could feel Louisa's scornful eyes on him, but he did not want to look at her or any of the Mahaffeys.

How could he have allowed this to happen? One of those men had been Sam Hawkins. There was no question of it. And the other must have been his brother, Ben, who, judging by his appearance, was certainly one of the three men who had run over Chet.

They were there, and he was there. The situation was just as he had wanted it to be, just as he had prayed it someday would be. He should have drawn his pistol and challenged them as he had dreamed of doing for more than a year now, but he had not been able to do it. He had stood there like a statue and been about as much use as one.

At the same time, he had allowed the Colonel to be robbed of the entire afternoon's take. He had always thought of himself as a man with a little bit of a backbone, but now he was beginning to wonder.

The Colonel did not appear to be too worried about his money. He was thinking about the two men that were still lying in the dirt near where the wagons had been.

"We've got to see if those men are alive, and if they are we must help them," he said. "Louisa, go look for Dr. Stuartson. Sophia, you and Mr. Storey come with me."

He stepped off the platform and started toward the men. His wife followed.

After a second's hesitation, so did Storey. His legs felt like wood, and he found it hard even to bend his knees. The answer to why he had not drawn his pistol began to dawn on him. It was obvious, and he knew he should have seen it sooner, but it was hard to admit such things to yourself.

He was a coward. His conception of himself as a sort of lone vigilante had been the worst sort of self-deception, the fantasy of a fool. He kicked at the ground in disgust.

The Colonel was kneeling beside one of the men, feeling for a pulse. Evidently, he found none.

"Dead," he said. "Shot in the back by those scurrilous poltroons. Men such as that have no reason for being in existence; they merely infest the earth like vermin."

He let the man's hand drop and moved to the other victim. This one seemed to be in better health, and Storey recognized him as the man he had seen in the dry goods store.

"It's Mr. Sanders," he said, correctly assuming that the name on the store was the name of its proprietor.

"You know him?" the Colonel said.

"Met him in town," Storey said.

"Well, he's a lucky man. It appears that the bullet struck him only a glancing blow on the side of his skull. He is unconscious, but his breathing is regular and steady. Dr. Stuartson should be able to patch him up right here."

"No, he won't," Louisa said. She was standing there with them. "Dr. Stuartson won't be able to do anything. He's in the back of the wagon, drunk as a lord."

"Drunk?" the Colonel said. "But he knows the rules about that!"

"Maybe he just didn't care," Louisa said. "I think he got into the alcohol you use for the miracle oil."

"My God," Sophia said. "He'll kill himself."

The Colonel's face was grim. "Not if I get to him first, my dear."

He turned to Storey. "My wife and I will go assist Dr. Stuartson. Perhaps we can get him into a passable condition. Meanwhile, you and Louisa might move this man into a better light so that we can clean his wound. If Dr. Stuartson is unable to help him, we may have to do so ourselves."

"Shouldn't someone go for the sheriff?" Storey said.

"I should think that any number of people have already informed the sheriff of our visitors," the Colonel said. "If they did not trample one another in there eagerness to leave here, that is."

Storey might have imagined it, but he thought the Colonel gave him a look of mild rebuke as he spoke, but without saying more, the Colonel and his wife went to the wagon, and Storey found himself alone with Louisa and the still unconscious Sanders.

It was not a situation that Storey relished. He had not been comfortable around Louisa for some time now.

It was not that she wasn't pretty; she was, and he was well aware of it. Too well aware. He had had other things on his mind up to this point, however, and his plans did not include getting tied down by some pretty young woman. He had been looking for Sam Hawkins.

Well, now he had found Hawkins, and he had found himself wanting. No one had yet said anything to him, but he could see what Louisa was thinking. It was plain on her face.

"We can't jostle him," he said, referring to Sanders, not looking Louisa in the eye. "I'll get my hands under his shoulders and you take his feet. We'll carry him to the tent."

Sanders was not particularly heavy, and they got him into the tent with no trouble. There were two benches there so that some of the men attending the anatomy lecture could be seated in relative comfort. They laid Sanders on the bench nearest the lantern.

Storey started to leave the tent, but Louisa's voice stopped him before he could escape. "You had a gun," she said. "Why didn't you use it? Why did you let those men get away with that woman and the money?"

Storey wanted to tell the truth, wanted to say that he had simply been unable to do anything, but something else suddenly occurred to him.

"I couldn't use the pistol," he said. "I didn't reload it after the shooting exhibition."

The worst thing about it was that he was telling the truth. He never reloaded after the exhibition, and all of them knew it. But even though it was true, it was still a lie.

"You could have made them believe that it was loaded," Lousia said, but she seemed less sure of herself now.

Hating himself even more, Storey said, "What if they didn't care? What if they'd shot all of us? I couldn't take that chance."

"I see," Louisa said, and Storey was surprised to see a glistening in her eyes that might have been the beginning of tears. "But I still think you should have done something!"

Storey was going to ask what he could have done, but she went on. "You could surely have stopped them from taking that woman if you had just stepped forward."

Storey was finding plenty of reason for self-disgust. He had forgotten all about the woman, worrying about his own problems.

"We'll tell the sheriff about her," he said, looking down at Sanders, who seemed to be stirring a bit. "Don't let him fall off the bench."

"And where are you going?"

"To check on Dr. Stuartson."

"That won't be necessary," the Colonel said, as he and his wife entered the tent, supporting The Boozer between them.

The Boozer did not look well, especially by lantern light. His face was not its usual brick red; it was instead a pasty shade of gray, and he could have used a shave. His knees were wobbly, and his hands were shaking even more than was usual for him.

"The Colonel administered a vomit to Dr. Stuartson," Sophia explained. "I believe that he has disgorged a rather large quantity of alcohol."

"A trifle," The Boozer said, his voice barely audible. "A mere trifle." He wiped the back of a trembling hand across his mouth.

"Can you look at the wounded man?" the Colonel said.

"Of course. Where is he?"

The question was not one that would have inspired confidence in Sanders had he heard it, since he was lying in plain sight not more than six feet away.

"Right here," Louisa said, pointing.

"Uh, oh. Of course. Let me look at him." The Boozer tried to take a few steps without support and folded at the knees.

Storey stepped to help him up, but moved back at a look from the Colonel. The Boozer knelt in the dirt for a moment, swaying slightly. Then he fell on his face.

This time Storey did help him up and held him erect.

"No good," The Boozer said. "I'm just . . . no good."

"Don't say such things," the Colonel told him. "You are a good man and a good doctor."

"Once," The Boozer said. "Was once. Not now."

"You are," the Colonel said. "You simply need to regain your confidence."

"No. No use. No use to anybody. Le'me go." He tried to pull away from Storey's grip.

"Very well," the Colonel said. "Release him, Mr. Storey."

Ray let go of The Boozer's arm, and the old man staggered out of the tent.

"Well?" Louisa said. "What do we do now?"

"As I said, the man's wound is not serious," the Colonel said. "I will treat it myself. Then we will see about getting Mr. Sanders back to town. I expect the sheriff will be here soon."

He left the tent to get some of his alcohol to use as an antiseptic.

Storey could feel Louisa looking at him, but she had nothing more to say now that her mother was with them. Ray felt his chest tighten, as if the air in the tent was beginning to suffocate him.

"I think I'll go outside for a minute," he said. "Someone should check on The Boozer."

"Don't call him that!" Louisa said.

"Sorry," Storey said, and then he escaped from the tent.

Coy Wilson found it hard to believe what he was hearing. Was it possible that Sam and Ben could have been so stupid?

It appeared that they could, at least according to Carl Gary, who stood in front of Wilson's desk in the little one-cell jail, his moustache fairly bristling with indignation. There was a mob of other irate citizens just outside backing him up.

"Two men, Sheriff," Gary said. "At least two. I saw them fall myself, shot in the back like dogs. And God knows what may have happened to those medicine show people by now. Those two women. . . . I hate to think what those animals might do to those women."

"You're sure it was the Hawkinses?" Wilson said. Dammit, the brothers had always been smart enough to avoid having any reliable witnesses before this. Why had they made such a mess of things this time?

"Of course it was them. You needn't try to get out of doing your duty by bringing out that tired old excuse. I saw them. Everyone saw them."

"And you didn't do anything to stop them?"

Gary paused and drew himself up straight. "What is it that you would have us do, Sheriff? We did as much as you have done against those two."

Gary was right, and Wilson could see that it would do no good to try and sidetrack him.

"We demand that you form a posse and go after them," Gary went on. "Now. Tonight."

Wilson wasn't eager for a posse. He had planned to go alone. There was danger that someone besides the two men Gary was talking about would be shot if a posse went out, and Wilson didn't think the Hawkins brothers were likely to be the ones who got hurt.

"I'd better ride out there to that show and check on things first," Wilson said. "See if they killed anybody else. We got to know exactly how much damage they did. Besides, it's not a good idea to go ridin' in on anybody like the Hawkinses in the dark. Best wait for daylight."

Gary saw the logic of the last part. In fact, he was pleased to hear it. He didn't actually want to be a part of a posse at all, much less at night, and he suspected that the others felt pretty much the same. But they had asked him to speak for them, and he had to put up a good front.

"You will form a posse?" he said. "You will ride on the Hawkins brothers in the morning as soon as it's light?"

"I can't make any promises like that," Wilson said, standing up.

"I got to see if things happened like you said. Then we'll see about what to do." He started around the desk.

Gary stepped aside to let Wilson get by. "Very well," he said. "Suppose you tell those people out there what your plans are. They are the ones I am representing, and it is their decision."

"Nope," Wilson said. "I'm the sheriff. It's my decision."

Wilson had never been fond of Gary. He seemed to think he had the right to tell everyone what to do since he was the wealthiest man in town. The sheriff wondered how many of the people outside the jail knew that Gary was always the most prompt when it came time to pay off the Hawkinses. The saloon owner didn't want to take any chances of getting his own place of business shot up, and he could afford to pay off even if the others couldn't. The Hawkins brothers had hardly affected him at all, if the truth were known.

Wilson stepped out the door and told the crowd what he was planning to do. There was a minute or two of muttering, but then everyone seemed to agree that it might be just as well to wait until morning.

"And another thing," Wilson said.

"What's that?" someone said.

"I won't be needin' a posse in the mornin'. I'll be ridin' out there alone."

"You must be crazy," Gary said from behind him. "Those men will kill you at once."

"Maybe they will, and maybe they won't. Anyway, that's my look-out. I'm the sheriff, and I'm doin' this my way."

Gary shrugged. If Wilson wanted to get himself shot to death, so be it. That way, Gary wouldn't have to risk his own life.

"What if you do get kilt?" a man asked. "Where the hell does that leave the rest of us?"

"Needin' a new sheriff, I reckon," Wilson said. "Now if you gents will let me get to my horse, I think I'll go out to that medicine show and see what the damage is."

"Two dead men, is what the damage is," the man said. "We all saw 'em fall. Barclay Sanders is one of 'em."

"Maybe they aren't dead," Wilson said moving through the crowd and freeing his horse's reins from the hitch rail. "Maybe they're just wounded."

He hoped he was right, but he suspected the man was right. He knew Ben and Sam too well. It wouldn't have bothered Sam at all to kill a fleeing man. For that matter, it wouldn't have bothered Ben, either.

"They fell like they was dead," another man said. "One of 'em didn't even holler. Just pitched on his face and slid."

The sheriff put his left foot in the stirrup and threw his right across the saddle.

"We'll see," he said pulling the reins and turning his horse's head. "We'll see."

Chapter Nine

Naomi thought that she was going to be sick.

She was bouncing up and down and the smells surrounding her were awful. There was the smell of horse and the smell of unwashed man. The second smell was worse.

Her head was hanging downward, and she could see the rising and the falling of the dark ground.

The only thing that kept her from vomiting was that she was so disoriented. She knew that the motion, the smell, the sound of hoofbeats, and the trees rushing by her in the darkness must mean that she was lying across a horse, but she didn't know how she had gotten there, or why.

She tried to raise her head, and someone slapped her on the rump.

"Hot damn, Sam, she's awake," said a man's voice that Naomi did not recognize.

Suddenly she remembered what had happened: the two men on their horses, the gunfire. She remembered fainting.

When she realized that somehow the men must have taken her, she began to struggle frantically.

"She's got gumption," the man said, pressing his hand down hard on the small of her back to hold her where she was lying in front of the saddle. "I like a woman that fights back."

"Me too, Ben," another voice said. It must be the man called Sam, Naomi thought. "Now shut up and let's get on back home."

But Ben didn't want to shut up. "How much money you reckon we got, Sam?"

"Fifty or sixty dollars," Sam said. "Couldn't have been more than that."

"Did you see those bastards scatter? I bet they thought we was gonna shoot ever' one of 'em."

"Yeah," Sam said. "They scattered, all right. All but two of 'em."

Ben laughed. "Hell, they won't be scatterin' for a long time. They're dead as that terrapin."

Naomi stopped struggling to think about the implications of what she had heard. She had not seen anyone shot, but she had been too frightened to look around. What if Lawton had been one of those who was killed? Who would come after her then?

For she never doubted that if he was alive her husband would come looking for her. She had learned that he was not a passionate man, but he was surely not the kind to allow his wife to be carried off by outlaws of the worst sort to suffer a fate worse than death.

"Oh dear!" she said aloud. She had just realized who Sam and Ben were.

"You say somethin', honey?" Ben asked.

Naomi did not answer. She was thinking about the sermon Lawton had preached about the Hawkinses. How she had admired him then! He had let the townspeople know where their duty lay, and preaching to them that way had been the most intrepid act her husband had ever performed. She had been a bit surprised. She had not known he had it in him.

Then she thought about the results of the sermon and of the way the Hawkinses had responded. The church had been badly damaged, and Lawton had not done a thing about it. It was as if his sermon had taken all of his courage and there was no more to replace it with.

She experienced an abrupt chill, as if the night had turned suddenly cold.

What if Lawton didn't come? What if she were left alone with the Hawkins brothers?

She pushed the thought from her mind. There were some things that simply didn't bear thinking about.

The Reverend Lawton Stump felt the same way, but he was thinking about his wife just the same. No matter how hard he tried not to think of her, his thoughts would take no other direction.

He was on his knees at the alter of his church, his eyes squeezed shut, his hands clasped in an attitude of prayer, his chin resting on his hands, but it was no good. He could not pray.

He stood up and looked around the church at the empty pews, at the moonlight streaming through the windows. In one place the moonlight was colored by the remaining bit of stained glass.

My God, the reverend Stump thought. *Those men have my wife.*

Panic filled him, and he ran to the door of the church, wrenched it open, and bolted into the street. The bright moonlight cast long shadows in front of the church and across the yard of Stump's house.

Down the way, the crowd was breaking up in front of the jail as Wilson rode down the street in the direction of the clearing where the show had been held.

Stump knew more or less what had been going on at the jail. The men had been assembled there when he got back to the church, but he had not joined them. Now he was surprised to see that Wilson was riding away alone.

He walked toward the jail until he saw Carl Gary. Calling out to him, he motioned for the saloon owner to join him.

Gary quickly explained the situation, and the panic that threatened to overwhelm Stump increased with every word. If the sheriff was not going to confront the Hawkinses until morning, what did that mean for Naomi?

"Two men were killed?" Stump said. "Nothing else?"

"Nothing else." Gary said. "Why, isn't that enough?"

Stump did not know what to say. Apparently no one but him had seen Naomi being taken by Sam and Ben. Having kept his silence until now, he feared to break it. Everyone would ask him why he had done nothing to prevent the taking of his wife.

"Yes," he said. "That's enough." He didn't know what else to say.

He left Gary and went back inside the church, but his mind was as restless as before. He could not concentrate on his prayers; his thoughts kept returning to his wife.

He was filled with regret. He had never been able to be a real husband to Naomi because he had been consumed by guilt, a guilt that he suddenly realized had been caused by an excess of love for her. He had been afraid that if he gave in to his love for a woman, his love for his church and his religion would be lessened, and he had let his normal human feelings be suppressed by his guilt.

He had been stupid.

Then he had cowered in hiding like a rabbit when two men had abducted his wife. He felt an even more intolerable guilt when he perceived that for a moment he might actually have wanted them to take her. If she were gone, there would be no more conflict in his mind about where his love and loyalty should lie.

Could he really have sunk that low? It appeared that he could, and as he sat on the back row of the church, looking forward at the simple altar and feeling the hard back of the seat pressing against his spine, he knew he would have to do something about it. His shoulders slumped. He could no longer serve his calling if he allowed himself to continue feeling about himself as he did, and if anything happened to Naomi, he would never forgive himself.

God could forgive anything, Stump knew that. But sometimes you needed more than God's forgiveness. You needed your own, too, and more than that you needed the forgiveness of other people, just as he needed Naomi's forgiveness. He hoped that she would be able to give it.

And he hoped that he would be able to receive it.

Ray Storey found The Boozer leaning against the same tree where he had rested earlier in the day and blithely saluted the mules and told them how wonderful life was.

The Boozer was not blithe now. Tears ran down his cheeks and sparkled in the moonlight. Storey thought first that it had been a long time since he had seen a moon so bright. Then he thought about the tears.

"Useless ol' man," The Boozer said. "Jus' a useless ol' man."

Storey would have liked to help The Boozer, to tell him that he wasn't useless at all but that he was a valuable member of the medicine show team, but he didn't see any point in lying. When you got right down to it, The Boozer's self-pitying judgment was pretty much on the money. He didn't do a damn thing except lend a bogus air of legitimacy to the show, and no matter what the Colonel thought, Storey did not believe that The Boozer was capable of performing so simple a task as the anatomy lecture.

At the same time, Storey knew that he was in no position to criticize. "You're no more useless than I am," he said.

The Boozer looked up, surprised that anyone was around. He had thought his remarks were being made to himself only.

"Not true," he said.

"It's true, all right," Storey said, thinking of the way he had stood there and how he had not been able to move his hand toward his gun. What difference did it make that the gun had not been loaded? He could not have drawn it even if it had.

"Not true," The Boozer repeated. He held up his shivering hands. "I used to be able to help people with these. Sick people. Now they're no good at all. No good." He sank back against the tree, letting his hands drop into his lap.

Storey reached down, intending to help The Boozer to his feet, but when his hand touched Stuartson's shoulder the old man shook it off.

"Go 'way," he said. "Jus' go 'way."

"You can't stay out here all night," Storey said. "You'll get sick."

The Boozer didn't answer. He just sat there, staring off into the trees. The silent tears were still flowing.

Storey looked at him in silence for a minute and then left him there.

"I can't see why Ray didn't do something," Louisa said. "He just stood right there and let them ride off with that woman. He could have done *something.*"

She was standing with her parents between the tent and the show wagon. Lantern light not much brighter than the moonlight spilled out of the tent and the back of the wagon.

"He told you that his gun had not been reloaded, did he not?" the Colonel said. "There was nothing he could have done."

That wasn't the answer Louisa wanted to hear.

"Those men spit at me," she said. "They shot at your feet. What if they had taken Mother or me? Would he have stood by and watched that, too? And why didn't he go after them? That poor woman—"

"You could ask him yourself," Sophia said. "Here he comes now."

Louisa turned to look, and Ray felt her eyes on him. He was pretty sure he knew what she was thinking about him, since he was thinking more or less the same thing himself.

"How's Mr. Sanders?" he said, avoiding the topic he figured they had been discussing.

"I cleansed the wound," the Colonel said. "It doesn't appear to be serious, but he is still unconscious. Where is Dr. Stuartson?"

"Sulking in the woods," Storey said.

"Oh!" Louisa said. "I don't see how you can talk like that about Dr. Stuartson. I'm sure that if I had behaved like you did, I wouldn't have anything snide to say about anyone else."

"Now, Louisa," Sophia said.

Louisa turned to her mother. "Don't try to keep me quiet, Mother. You know very well that Dr. Stuartson has had a sad life and that he's not to blame for his drinking. At least he has an excuse, which is more than you can say for some people."

She looked at Storey again with her last words and then turned and walked away, her back stiff.

"She's a bit upset by the events of the evening," the Colonel said.

"So I see," Storey said. He felt awkward and ungainly and stupid in his buckskins, not knowing what to do or say. How could he explain himself? What excuse could he offer?

He was saved from saying more by the arrival of Coy Wilson.

"I hear you had a little trouble out of the Hawkins brothers," Wilson said when he had dismounted and introduced himself.

"Is that who they were?" the Colonel said. "They did not offer formal introductions."

"I can understand that," Wilson said. "But they were identified by a number of witnesses. Folks around here have had trouble out of 'em before." He shook his head. "That's who they were all right."

"Those witnesses," the Colonel said. "I imagine that they told you about the men who were shot."

Wilson nodded. "Dead, both of 'em, is what I hear."

"Not both," Storey said. "Mr. Sanders is alive. He's in the tent there."

"What about the other one?"

"Oh, he's dead all right," the Colonel said. "He's still lying where he fell. We have not had time to move him inside as yet. But what do you intend to do about the woman?"

"What woman?" Wilson said.

"The one those men took away from here," Sophia said. "They carried her away with them."

Goddammit, Wilson thought. *This is gettin' worse and worse.* He had hoped for a minute that things weren't as bad as he had feared. Only one man dead instead of two. That wasn't so bad. Things had been looking up. And now they were talking about some woman being carried away. Sam and Ben must have gone plumb crazy.

"Who was she?" he said.

No one knew. Storey was able to describe her fairly well, however, having seen her in town and remembering that she was the only woman still there. Besides, she had bought some of the Miracle Oil from him, and he wasn't likely to forget that.

"Sounds like Naomi Stump," Wilson said. "The preacher's wife." His mind was racing. Everything he heard unnerved him more. What the hell had the preacher's wife been doing here, anyway? Didn't she have enough sense to know not to come to a medicine show?

"The preacher's wife?" the Colonel said. "I imagine that will cause a bit of trouble in town, especially if she is harmed."

Trouble was right. Wilson dreaded having to tell the preacher. But if no one else had seen her taken, maybe he wouldn't have to tell anyone, not if he could get her back before anything happened to her.

That meant he was going to have to go out there before morning and convince the Hawkins brothers to let the woman go and get out of there. If he could. Sam and Ben might not want to give the woman up so soon, and they might not want to go.

It almost seemed as if they were intent on ruining his plans, though there was no way they could know what those plans were. They did not yet know that it was not his plan to return to Kansas with them.

He knew that most of the townspeople did not like him, that they thought he was a bully who liked to push them around, and maybe he had been a little uppity with them from time to time. Living here had changed him, however. He could see that he no longer wanted to live on the wrong side of the law. In playing the part of a lawman, he had decided that he liked the job and wanted to do more than play it. He'd done a lot of things wrong in his life, the worst being running down that kid, but maybe he could make up for a few of them if he stayed on and did a good job of lawing.

Sam and Ben wouldn't undersand that; they wouldn't undersand that at all. So he wasn't going to tell them. He was just going to let them have the money and go on their way. He would look good to the town, and they would be gone. Life would be pretty easy after that.

Or it would have been if Sam and Ben had gone along with the scheme he had laid out for them. Now it was looking more and more as if they were deliberately trying to mess him up.

"What do you think, Sheriff?" the Colonel said, drawing Wilson out of his meditations.

"I think I'm going to have to ride out to the Hawkins boys' place and see if I can talk some sense into 'em," Wilson said.

"Talking won't bring back that man over there," the Colonel said, looking over to where the body still lay.

"It won't help that woman they took, either," Louisa said. She had walked back and joined the group to hear what the sheriff had to say.

"I reckon I might have to do more than talk, then," Wilson said.

"And you plan to go up against them alone?" Louisa said. She was looking at Wilson, but Storey knew who the words were aimed at.

"Yep," Wilson said. "I won't need no help against those two." He hoped that he wasn't lying. If Sam and Ben decided to cross him, he was in big trouble. It would take more than him to get them then. It might take more than the whole town.

Chapter Ten

Sam and Ben weren't going along with Wilson's plan. They had talked it over after they shoved the woman in their one-room house and shut the door, warning her not to try to escape.

"Shoot you if you do," Ben warned her. "It wouldn't mean no more to me that it would to shoot that damn cat."

The cat was sitting on the porch watching them when they rode up. Naomi thought she had never seen a more miserable cat, and she forgot her own troubles for a moment as she looked at it. Its hair was sparse and thin; she could see patches of skin where there was no hair at all. She wondered where the cat had come from and why it stayed there.

She did not want to go inside the house, but Ben dragged her up on the porch, slapped her, and pushed her through the door, sending her sprawling.

She fell heavily inside and lay still for a moment. The smell in there was worse than it had been on the horse, and the floor was covered in filth. She sat up and wiped her hands on her dress.

The moonlight came in through the one empty window and made

a pool of brightness on the floor, crosshatched by the shadows of the pine limbs.

Naomi could see the outlines of two ragged corn shuck mattresses, a rickety table and two chairs that looked as if they could collapse any second, and a shelf that held a tiny supply of canned goods and a sack of flour. That was all. The Hawkinses didn't go in for high living.

Naomi took the threat of shooting seriously, and she was not yet ready to attempt an escape. She was sure that her husband would come, and if he did not, Kit Carson, that strong young man from the medicine show would come. She knew that a big man like that must be courageous and possess a sense of justice. Surely he would not allow the Hawkinses to get away with taking her away as they had done.

For now, there seemed to be nothing for her to do except wait for rescue. At least the two men had not actually tried to do her any harm as she had feared they might. Maybe they would not molest her after all. Maybe they were worried about her husband, or about Kit Carson.

She moved to the door and put her ear against it. She hoped to overhear the Hawkins brothers and get some idea about their plans for her.

Ben and Sam weren't worried about Lawton Stump, Kit Carson, or anyone else. They had seen the townspeople scattering like rats at the medicine show, and they had seen the way the men in the buckskins was afraid to stand up to them. Sheriff Coy Wilson was no threat; he was on their side.

"He sounded kind a funny today, though," Ben said, after listening for a minute at the door to make sure that there was no ruckus from inside the house. "You reckon he really thinks he can run us off if we don't want to go?"

"He knows better than that," Sam said. He reached inside his shirt and pulled out the sack of money. "Let's see what we got us here."

He opened the bag and they sat down on the porch to count the money. The moon was easily bright enough for them to do the job. The cat sat and watched them with indifference, now and then scratching vigorously at its ears with one or the other of its back feet.

"Sixty-three dollars," Sam said. "I thought damn near ever'body in town musta bought some of that fake medicine, and all we got here is sixty-three dollars."

"Yeah," his brother agreed. "Sixty-three dollars sure ain't much for a night's work. The way Coy talked, I'd have thought we'd get a hunnerd dollars easy."

Sam was beginning to get mad. The more he thought about things, the less he liked the way Wilson had talked to them that afternoon, as if he was trying to tell them what they had to do. Wilson had been a part of the gang, but he hadn't been the boss. They had all been equals.

"Seems like Coy's gettin' a little big for his britches here lately," Sam said.

Ben nodded quickly. He'd been thinking that for a good while. "Seems like we take all the risks, and he gets most of the money. All he has to do is fool folks into thinking he's a real sheriff. We're the ones that might get shot at."

Sam thought so, too. True, they hadn't been at much of a risk at any time, and the money had come easily, but it did seem like they were the ones doing all the work.

"And now he thinks he can tell us just to move on," Ben went on. "Hell, if it wasn't for him runnin' down that kid, we wouldn't be stuck down here in goddamn Texas in the first place. He thinks we ought to pick up and leave just because he's lettin' us have a whole sixty-three dollars."

Naomi was able to hear most of what was said. The door did not exactly fit the frame, and there was a fairly large crack through which the men's voices carried clearly.

She did not know what to make of all she heard, but it was clear that Sheriff Wilson and the Hawkins brothers were in league with one another. No wonder the sheriff had never taken any action against them!

But there was more. Something about the sheriff telling them to leave. She fervently hoped they would do so, and that they would do it soon.

Sam wasn't inclined to leaving, however. "Coy might think he can take over the town for himself," he said. "That'd be just about his style. Get rid of us and have it all to himself."

"I bet that's it," Ben said. "I bet he wants to get rid of us some way. I bet he ain't even plannin' to go with us back to Kansas."

"Sometimes you're smarter than you look, Ben," Sam told him, thinking over what his brother had said. It made sense. Old Coy was going to try making himself look like a hero by running the Hawkins boys out of town, and then he was going to settle down and live the high life. In the meantime, Sam and Ben were supposed to hang their heads and ride back to Kansas like good little boys.

"We ain't gonna do it, though," Sam said.

"Do what?" Ben said.

"Go back to Kansas like good little boys."

"Why not? I'm ready to go back, and that's the God's truth. I'm tired of this damn place. Look at those trees there." He gestured at the tall pines that virtually surrounded them. "It ain't natural to have all those trees growin' around a man's house."

The cat, having lost all interest in the conversation, went to the edge of the porch, jumped down, and disappeared around the side of the house without so much as meowing. If it had learned nothing else, it knew that it paid to keep your mouth shut around the Hawkins brothers.

"Coy's tryin' to get rid of us all right," Sam said. "But we ain't gonna let him. Before we leave here, we're gonna show this town what the Hawkins boys can do when they get riled. And we're gonna get more than a piddlin' sixty-three dollars out of it, too."

Ben didn't know what Sam was planning, but that didn't matter. He was always willing to go along with Sam's ideas, since they were usually good ones. They were a damn sight better than any ideas Ben ever had.

"What about the woman, then?" Ben said.

"Yeah," Sam said, smiling. "What about her?"

When Wilson rode away from the show wagon, the Colonel and Storey moved the dead man inside the tent. Storey usually slept in the tent, and so did The Boozer, but Storey wasn't sure he wanted to sleep there tonight.

Someone had to stay with Mr. Sanders, however, in case he woke up, and Storey agreed to do so.

The Mahaffeys went to the wagon, and Storey could hear them engaged in a heated discussion. He hoped that he was not the subject.

He was not. Sophia Mahaffey was trying to convince her husband that they should leave the site as soon as the sun rose and make their way for another town.

"I had a bad feeling about this place all along," she said, voicing the foreboding she had experienced that day. She did not remind her husband that he had expected to have a very successful show.

"We are not leaving," the Colonel said. "We promised those people tonight that we would do another show tomorrow, and so we shall." His blue eyes snapped. "I am not going to let two common ruffians deter me from giving my performances."

"But we have no protection," Louisa said.

"What do you mean?" he father said. "We have Mr. Storey. He has a gun."

"Ha," Louisa said.

"You are too hasty to judge," the Colonel said, eyeing his daughter and noting the way the mention of Storey's name brought the color to her cheeks. "You refused to let Mr. Storey make idle comments about Dr. Stuartson, but you are quite ready to pass judgment on Mr. Storey. How are we to know that he has not suffered as much as Dr. Stuartson? Or even more?"

"Ha," Louisa said again. She didn't believe for a minute that Ray Storey knew the meaning to the word "suffer." How could someone so young have suffered? All she knew was that he had stood by and let things happen all around him, terrible things. He had betrayed her image of him, and she was not likely to forgive him easily.

"I think it might be time for you to have a talk with your daughter, Sophia," the Colonel said.

"Oh, she's my daughter, is she?" Sophia's eyes snapped. "And why can't you be the one to have a talk with her?"

"I have to prepare for tomorrow's show," the Colonel said. "I have to make sure we have enough Miracle Oil and Vitality Pills."

"I'll help you with that tomorrow," Sophia said. "That is, if you're sure we can't just leave here. It's bad luck. I can feel it. Please. Let's leave with first light."

"I do not believe in luck," the Colonel said. "I believe in hard work and good medicine. With those two things we can overcome all adversity."

"I'd like to see medicine overcome two men with pistols," Louisa said.

"Sophia," the Colonel said. "Speak to her."

Ray Storey sat on one of the benches and looked at the two men, only one of whom was breathing. He told himself that he was not responsible for the death of the one or the injury to the other, but for some reason he kept thinking of Chet, the way Chet's eyes had looked just before the horse trampled him that hot summer day.

There was something in that look, something that was as hard to explain as it was to forget.

It was more than the boy's fear, though that was part of it. There was something else that had haunted Storey ever since. It was a plea, almost a demand.

"Help me," the look said. "Help me."

I tried, dammit, Story thought. *I tried, Chet.*

But he had not tried tonight. He had done nothing. He had watched and done nothing.

Barclay Sanders stirred, moving his head and turning his body like a restless sleeper as he came out of his stupor. Storey got up and walked over to the storekeeper.

"It's all right, Mr. Sanders," he said. He put a hand on Sanders's shoulder to keep him from sitting up too quickly.

"Wha' . . . Where?" Sanders's voice was thick. His eyes wouldn't quite focus.

"You're in the medicine show tent," Storey said. "You had a pretty good knock in the head." He didn't want to try explaining that Sanders had been shot. That could come later.

Sanders swung his legs around slowly and sat up, with Storey's help. His head was throbbing, and he lowered it into his hands.

"You'll be fine," Storey said. "You just sit here for a while. I'll tell the Colonel that you're awake. He'll put some Miracle Oil on your head, and you'll be fine in no time."

Sanders was feeling dizzy; unable to speak, he waved Storey away. Storey went to the wagon. He knocked at the door frame, and Louisa opened the door.

"What do you want?" she said, looking straight into his eyes.

Storey hoped he was imagining the emphasis she put on the word "you," but he didn't think he was. The emphasis was there in the eyes, too.

"Mr. Sanders is awake," he said. "The Colonel might ought to have a look at him."

"I'll tell him," Louisa said. "Thank you." She shut the door sharply and left Storey standing there looking at it.

He resisted the impulse to take off his hat and throw it at the ground. Instead, he turned and walked to the trees where he had hobbled his horse.

He had to do something. It didn't matter to him if he got killed or not. He couldn't stand the look in Louisa's eyes anymore.

That was funny when he thought about it. Until tonight, he hadn't cared one way or another about what Louisa thought, though it had been pretty obvious that she liked him more than a little. Now that she hated him, it seemed that her opinion was more important than anything. It was bad enough that he despised himself, but somehow having her despise him was more than he could stand.

His saddle trappings and blanket were under a tree near his horse.

The mules were nearby, and they watched him with a sleepy curiosity. He put the blanket across the horse's back, pitched on the saddle, and tightened the girth.

Then he thought of something else he had better do. He reloaded the pistol, with real bullets and real lead this time. He didn't know if he would be able to use them, but by God he would at least deprive himself of the cowardly excuse he had used earlier.

Maybe he would be able to do something after all. He didn't have anything against that sheriff, but Wilson didn't look like the kind of man who could stand up against Sam and Ben Hawkins all alone. It wouldn't hurt him to have a little backing.

Storey climbed on the horse. He hoped that they got there in time to save the woman.

The Boozer watched Storey saddle the horse and load the pistol. The Boozer was a drunk, but at the moment his mind was clear. No one had to tell him where Storey was going. There was nobody better than him at being able to tell when a man was feeling useless, and unlike The Boozer himself, Storey was still young enough and fool enough to think that there was something he could do about it.

The Boozer watched Storey ride away. *What the hell*, The Boozer thought. *If he can try to do something about it, why can't I?*

He walked to one of the mules. "Why can't I, indeed?" he said.

The mule looked at him drowsily, twitching its ears.

The Boozer had been something of a horseman once, having ridden more than a few miles in visiting his patients, and he still remembered how to fashion a hackamore from a rope of the proper length. He looked around the outside of the tent until he found a piece that suited his needs. Before he went back to the mule, he paused a minute to listen to the voices he heard in the tent.

One of them belonged to the Colonel, and the other must be that of the wounded man. The Boozer felt a wave of futility wash over him. The man had been hurt, bleeding, and he had been able to do nothing to help him. He had been a doctor once; now he was nothing.

He walked back to the mules and talked quietly to Sunny, the one who was used to being ridden. Sunny had gotten its name from its disposition, which was pretty much the opposite of sunny, but The Boozer had always gotten along with the animal fairly well.

The Boozer constructed the hackamore with swift sureness, his hands betraying none of the tremors of only a short time before, and slipped it over Sunny's head.

"Life is no longer quite so wonderful," The Boozer said as he mounted the mule with more agility than anyone would have suspected possible by looking at him.

Sunny snorted and began plodding slowly in the direction that Ray Storey had taken.

"Life, in fact, gives off a strong odor of manure at the present moment," The Boozer said. "At least for some of us it does."

He looked up at the yellow brightness of the moon. "The world could be such a beautiful place, Sunny," he said. "Why is it that we make of it such a spittoon?"

The mule snorted again and twitched its ears.

"Precisely," The Boozer said, wondering vaguely what he hoped to accomplish by following Storey. Once, long ago, he had read a book about a man named Don Quixote, a man who had thought a heard of sheep was a mighty army and had fought them valiantly until the shepherds got to him and half killed him. Quixote had a squire, whose name The Boozer could not quite recall.

He thought that the squire had ridden a donkey, but it might just as well have been a mule.

Chapter Eleven

Lawton Stump had a pistol that he kept in the back of the bottom drawer of the chiffonier that stood against one wall of the bedroom. The pistol was an old Shopkeeper's Model Colt's Peacemaker, and it had never been fired. It had been given to Stump by his father, years before.

He still remembered what his father had told him. "You'll be preachin' in some places where nobody's gonna care whether you're a preacher or not, son. The time might come when you need this."

Stump had taken the gun from his father's hand and looked at it as if it were some strange, ugly animal that his father had offered him.

"I know you don't feel that way now," his father said. "But you never know when you might change your mind. You take it, and you and me both'll hope you never have to use it."

Stump had wrapped the shiny pistol in its flannel cover soon after that and more or less forgotten about it.

The gun had been shiny and new when he got it, but now its finish was dulled from the years of lying in the back of the drawer wrapped in a piece of red flannel. Stump had never even taken it out to practice with it.

It was not loaded, but there were six bullets wrapped in a separate piece of flannel. The bullets had been in the gun when he received it from his father, and he had never bought more. He had, in fact, thought it a foolish gift, and he had certainly never intended to use it.

There was no corrosion on the bullets that Stump could see, and he thumbed them into the chambers. He closed the cylinder and hefted the pistol in his hand. It was surprisingly heavy, and he wondered if he could hold it steady to fire it. Well, he would soon find out.

Stump did not have a saddle horse, but he had a buggy and a horse to pull it. Both were kept at the livery stable, and Stump knew that Rook Peterson, who owned the stable and lived next door to it, wasn't going to like having to get up in the middle of the night to let Stump in and hitch up the horse, but that was too bad. Stump paid a goodly sum each month for the care and feeding of the horse and the storage of the buggy. Peterson would just have to be upset.

Stump wasn't exactly sure why he had left the church and gone home for the pistol. He just knew that he had to do something about his wife, and that he could not wait until morning as Carl Gary had told him the sheriff was planning to do. He had to do something tonight, because he was sure that the Hawkinses would not wait until morning to do something to Naomi.

He wished that he possessed the gumption to tell the sheriff about her, but he didn't. To do so would have been too humiliating, and now he had to do something to make up for his silence, not only to the sheriff but at the medicine show earlier. He might have kept silent forever and no one the wiser, but his conscience would not let him rest if he did that.

It would not even allow him to pray.

He stuck the pistol into the belt below his hard belly and started to the livery stable.

The cat jumped in through the window, frightening Naomi as she listened at the door. She jumped back with a sharp intake of breath. She was quietly relieved when she saw the yellow cat looking at her from the puddle of moonlight.

The cat stared at her for a moment, then shook its tail and began walking around the room as if looking for something in the shadows. It stopped and sniffed at one of the mattresses, then at the other.

Naomi hoped that it was not looking for mice, but she would not have been surprised if the place were infested with them. There was really no place for them to hide, however, unless they were in the mattresses. She watched in silence as the cat made a circuit of the room.

When it was finished and satisfied that there was nothing for it to eat or stalk, it walked over to Naomi and rubbed against her skirts. She reached down and patted its head, hoping that it did not have mange.

The cat began purring. It was not used to any show of affection.

Naomi forgot her surroundings for a while and thought that she was like the cat in a way. If only Lawton would show her a little bit of fondness, she would purr for him in much the same way the cat was purring for her now.

She reached into her reticule, the drawstring of which she had somehow managed to hold onto throughout her whole ordeal. The Vitality Pills and the Miracle Oil were still there. She felt foolish now about having bought them, but at the same time she wondered how her life might change if the pills really did work, if they really were able to give to Lawton the spark of vitality that he seemed to be lacking.

The cat had stopped rubbing against her leg and walked over to the splash of moonlight, where he lay down on his stomach and began licking his front paws.

At that moment, Naomi heard someone ride up. She closed her reticule and walked over to the door, wondering if Lawton had arrived.

Coy Wilson, not Stump rode into the clearing.

Sam and Ben were sitting on the porch, silvered by the moonlight like two statues in a graveyard. If Wilson hadn't known better, he might have thought they had not moved since he had seen them earlier that day.

"Howdy boys," he said when he got near the porch.

"Howdy, Coy," Ben said. Sam didn't say anything.

"How'd things turn out at that medicine show?" Wilson said. He had no idea what the two men might say or do. They had not displayed good judgment at the medicine show, that much was for certain, and Wilson was no longer sure that he could predict their reactions to anything with certainty.

"Sixty-three dollars," Sam said. "Sixty-three damn dollars, Coy. That ain't much."

"I thought it'd be more," Wilson said. He had, too, having seen the prices on the handbill, but he hadn't known that the Colonel always gave away the Vitality Pills.

"Sixty-three dollars," Sam said again. "That ain't much to go to Kansas on, Coy."

"You've got a lot more than sixty-three dollars put away somewhere," Wilson said. "We've taken a lot more than that out of this town."

Naomi wondered about that and looked back at the room. One thing was for sure, and that was that the Hawkinses weren't spending a lot of money on themselves or their house. There wasn't much place to hide anything in the room, and she began to wonder where the money might be. She thought it might be a good idea to take it with her when the sheriff rescued her. Many of the people in town would appreciate it, and maybe even Lawton would think more of her.

She was mildly disappointed that Lawton had not shown up, but it was probably better that the sheriff had come. It was his job, anyway. But if he was working with the Hawkins brothers, would he really try to save her?

Nobody was thinking about her at the moment, however, so she forgot her fear and decided to look for the money. She would start with the shelf.

Outside, Wilson was still trying to find out where he stood

with the Hawkinses. He was sitting relaxed in his saddle, one hand holding the reins, the other not far from the pistol on his hip.

"You boys caused quite a ruckus out at that show tonight," he said.

"I guess we did, at that," Sam said.

"Killed a man," Wilson said.

Sam smiled. "Is that a fact. Hell, I thought it was two of them, Coy." He laughed, and Ben joined in.

"You're not the shot you were at one time, I guess," Wilson said. He wasn't laughing. "There wasn't any call to kill anybody."

"Wasn't any call not to," Sam said. Hell, it looked to him like Coy was getting soft in his old age. Maybe being a sheriff had started to affect his mind.

"Yeah," Ben said. "Wasn't any call not to. You startin' to fall in love with the sweethearts that live in this town, Coy?"

"It's not that," Wilson said. "It's just that I don't hold with killin' somebody who's not even shootin' at you."

"Don't recall you ever feelin' that way before, Coy," Sam said. "Don't recall that kid you ran down back up in Kansas shootin' at you, either."

"Damn you," Wilson said. "That was an accident."

"Accident or not, don't make no difference. It all works out the same," Sam said.

Coy was tired of the argument. "You're right, it don't make no difference now. All that matters is now is that it's time for you and Ben to light a shuck from here. Go on back to Kansas. We've milked this business for all it's worth.

"Well, now," Sam said. "Does that mean you ain't goin' with us, Coy?"

"I guess it does," Wilson said.

"Sure," Sam said. "You come out here, we leave, and ever'body thinks you're some kinda hero. Well, I don't think it's gonna work out exactly that way, Coy."

"Yeah," Ben said. "It ain't gonna work out exactly that way. See,

Sam and me, we got us somethin' more than money out at that show tonight."

Wilson had been wondering when they were going to get around to that.

"Got you a woman, I hear," he said.

"That's right," Sam said. "Ben, he wanted to take her and I didn't see any reason why not."

"You might've thought about how folks in town would feel about it," Wilson said.

"Hell, we don't care about that," Sam said. "Do we, Ben?"

"Hell, no," Ben said, laughing.

"I think you're gonna have to give her up, boys," Wilson said.

"Thought you might say that," Sam told him. "We ain't plannin' to do it, though."

In the shack, Naomi was at the door listening again. She had already found the money. It had been in the flour sack, and she had begun to think how happy everyone would be when it was returned to them. Now she was afraid again. It seemed as if the sheriff were on her side, but Sam and Ben were not about to give in to him.

"Boys," Wilson said, "we've rode some hard trails together and done a sight of things. Hell, we've seen the elephant. I'd hate to see us get off on the wrong foot about this woman."

"I never thought I'd see you go soft, Coy," Sam said. "I just never thought it."

"I ain't gone soft. I've just got some sense, finally, and if you had any you'd see I'm tellin' you the truth. I got to take the woman back, Sam."

Ben looked at his brother. "We ain't gonna let him, are we, Sam?" He didn't want to let the woman go. He had plans for the woman.

"No, Ben," Sam said. He wasn't smiling any more. "We ain't gonna let him."

Ray Storey had thought it would be easy to find the place where the Hawkins brothers lived, having gotten what he thought were pretty fair directions from the bartender that morning, but he wasn't familiar with the territory. He had skirted the town, and he was sure he was going in the right direction, but he hadn't been able to find the house.

Besides that, someone was following him.

He rode off the trail and into a stand of pine trees and waited quietly in the shadows. He could smell the bracing scent of the pines and hear bugs buzzing around his head. Off in the distance a mockingbird sang sleepily.

It wasn't long before The Boozer came along on Sunny. Storey could hear him talking to the mule.

"He went right along here," The Boozer said. "I saw him just a minute ago. We can't let him get away from us, Sunny."

Storey came out of the trees. "What are you doing here, Dr. Stuartson?" he said.

If Stuartson was surprised, he didn't show it. "Sunny and I were having a philosophical discussion," he said.

"It didn't sound too philosophical to me," Storey said. "It sounded like you were looking for somebody, most likely me."

"True, we were doing that, too," Stuartson said without apology. "We thought you might need some help when you got where you were going."

"And where might that be?" Storey thought as soon as he said it that he sounded just like that preacher he'd met in town, but it was too late to take it back.

"Looking for redemption," Stuartson said.

Storey could see The Boozer's eyes in the moonlight, and they were clear and sober. He didn't ask the doctor how he knew.

"I thought I might find some for myself," Stuartson added.

"Well, come on, then," Storey said. "I think the place I'm looking for is right around here. You might get shot, though. Those were some pretty rough fellas we met tonight."

"I'm not worried about getting shot," Stuartson said in a voice that seemed to imply he might welcome it. "Lead on."

It was just about then that the shooting began.

"Let's go," Storey said, setting his heels to his horse's ribs. The

Boozer followed after him as fast as Sunny would go.

Less than a quarter of a mile behind them, the Reverend Stump flicked the reins to urge his own horse to go faster, and the little buggy jumped ahead, dust pluming up into the moonlight from beneath its wheels. Stump thought he recognized the young man from the medicine show, but he wasn't sure who the other one was. Clearly, they were headed for the Hawkins place, which was where the shooting seemed to be coming from.

Stump tried to pray again, but he still received no comfort.

He reached down and touched the gun in his belt.

That made him feel better immediately.

Wilson should have seen it coming, but he didn't, not until it was too late. Ben and Sam both went for their guns at the same time, almost as if some signal had passed between them; but if it did, Wilson didn't see it.

One second they were sitting there, the moonlight slanting across them on the porch, and the next they were coming to their feet with their pistols drawn.

Wilson's horse reared as the first two shots were fired, causing the bullets to pass harmlessly by, and by then Wilson had his own pistol out.

Flame spurted from both the Hawkinses' guns before Wilson got off a shot. He jumped as if he'd been kicked by a mule as a bullet slammed into his shoulder, and his own shot went wild, crashing through the front wall of the cabin.

Naomi screamed and dropped to the floor, and the cat jumped up and ran under the table.

Wilson felt himself sliding off his horse, but he got off another shot before he fell. He didn't hit anyone that time, either. As soon as he hit the ground, he struggled to his feet and brought his gun up.

He didn't fire it. A bullet slapped into his side and spun him around. This time it was worse than a horse kicking. There was no pain, but it felt as if the jail had fallen on him. He fell again, and this time he didn't get up.

His horse walked a little way off to the side and stood there as if wondering what to do next.

Smoke swirled around the heads of the Hawkins brothers as they cleared spent cartridges from the cylinders of their pistols.

"Hate it that we had to kill old Coy like that," Ben said as he reloaded. "He was a good pardner till he got biggety with us about leavin' here." He looked out toward where Wilson lay and shook his head with regret. "Seems like we oughta do somethin' with him, not just leave him lyin' out there like that damn terrapin. It don't seem right, somehow."

"He won't care if we leave him there a while," Sam said. "We got other things to do." He gave a nod toward the door.

Ben's face lightened, his momentary sadness at shooting his former partner making an instant departure.

"Damn," he said. "When the shootin' started, I near 'bout forgot that woman. Who's gonna be first?"

Sam was feeling generous. "It was your idea to bring her. I guess you deserve first chance."

"That's mighty square of you, Sam," Ben said. He turned toward the door.

The shooting had terrified Naomi, but after finding herself still alive after the bullet had splintered the wall near her, she recovered quickly. She decided that she had best prepare herself for the worst, since there were two Hawkins brothers and only one sheriff. She didn't think that the sheriff had much of a chance.

She still hadn't quite figured out why the Hawkinses would want to kill the man they had worked with, though it seemed that he was trying to change for the better and send them on their way. Maybe that was it, but it didn't make any difference. She knew that once they were finished with the sheriff, they would be coming for her.

The trouble was that there didn't seem to be anything in the room to use as a weapon.

She looked around almost desperately. The chairs appeared flimsy, but when she tried, she found that she could not dismantle either of them. Almost as soon as she got her hands on them, the shooting stopped.

That left her with only one choice. She didn't want to do it, but it looked like her only chance.

"Damn that Lawton Stump," she said. Her husband would have been surprised to hear her curse him, she knew, but he should have been there by now.

The door swung open just as she picked up the cat.

It was hard to say which was more surprised, Ben or the cat that Naomi flung in his face.

Maybe the cat, since Naomi had shown it a bit of emotional warmth, something she had definitely not shown Ben.

The cat yowled as it flew through the air, claws extended. Only Ben's thick beard and hair saved him from an even more painful experience than the one he had as the cat scratched for a purchase on his head.

Ben bellowed and stumbled backward out the door and onto the porch, right into Sam, who had stood up to see what the hell was the matter.

Both men tottered on the edge of the porch, trying to balance themselves. They might have succeeded if Naomi had not pushed them.

She came dashing out the door as fast as she could run in her skirts and petticoats, clutching her reticule and the flour sack to her chest. When she saw Ben and Sam, she risked the reticule by flinging it outward, still holding onto the drawstring.

The reticule caught Ben a glancing blow on the temple, and not a very hard blow at that, but it was enough to overbalance him and Sam.

They toppled off the porch and landed on the hard ground, Ben smack on top of Sam, who had the breath knocked out of him in a loud gust.

The cat, which had clung to Ben's face throughout, sprang off and bowed its back, hissing and striking at Ben's beard with one of its front paws. Then it ran under the porch.

Naomi jumped off the porch just as the cat went under it. She started across the yard, holding her reticule and the flour sack in her right hand and hiking her skirts with her left.

Ben leaped off Sam and drew his pistol.

He was cocking the hammer when Storey and The Boozer pounded into the yard, followed closely by Lawton Stump in his buggy.

Chapter Twelve

Astonishingly, the Reverend Stump was the only one of the three men coming into the yard who had drawn a pistol.

The Boozer did not have a gun, however, so he had an excuse. Ray Storey did not.

Stump pulled back on the reins with his left hand. The horse planted its feet and came to a sudden stop, the buggy skidding sideways as Stump got off his first shot. The bullet whizzed over Ben's head and into the trees.

The sheriff's horse bolted in the midst of the excitement and ran behind the house, dragging its reins.

Ben's return shot was more accurate than Stump's, but not by much. It clipped a chunk out of the side of the buggy and sent it flying.

Sam was getting to his feet, drawing his own gun.

Storey headed his horse right at him, never slowing down.

Storey flashed by as Sam threw himself aside, landing on the porch and skidding to the doorway. Splinters dug into the soles of his palms.

"Goddamn!" he yelled.

Naomi sprinted across the yard toward her husband while The

Boozer calmly dismounted to see what, if anything, he could do for the fallen sheriff.

Naomi was almost to the buggy now. Stump fired over her head. The bullet went straight through the open door of the shack and exploded a can of tomatoes on the shelf. He fired again, sending a bullet into the door frame.

"Goddamn!" Sam yelled again. He crawled inside and slammed the door, right in the face of Ben, who was trying to get inside. The latch caught and held.

Ben hardly slowed. He turned and jumped off the end of the porch, heading for the ramshackle lean-to where he and Sam kept their horses.

He was hardly past the window when Sam jumped out right behind him.

"She took the goddamn money!" Sam said.

Ben didn't care. All he wanted to do right now was to get to the horses.

Out of the corner of his eye, Sam saw Wilson's horse near the lean-to. He veered off toward it.

The horse was still spooked, but though it danced back a step or two, it did not flee as Sam neared it. Sam grabbed the reins and saddle horn and swung himself onto the horse's back. He kicked the horse in the ribs and sped into the trees, leaning forward on the horse's neck.

Ben watched his brother go. "Son of a bitch, Sam," he said. "Don't run off and leave me."

Storey rounded the house, still not having drawn his pistol. Ben snapped off a quick shot at him and jumped on his own horse. He wrapped his arms around its neck and took off, his rear end bouncing up and down. Ben yelped all the way into the trees as tender parts of his anatomy came into contact with the horse's backbone.

Storey watched him go, knowing that he should go after him, but telling himself that it wouldn't do any good. The Hawkinses knew the lay of the land, and he didn't. They would likely ambush him and kill him before he got a half mile.

Anyway, even if he hadn't drawn his pistol, at least he hadn't been afraid to ride right at one of the Hawkinses, coming close to riding him down. He only wished that he had succeeded. There would have been a kind of justice in that.

He turned back to see if everyone else was all right.

Wilson was still alive.

He had been shot once in the shoulder and once in the side, but neither bullet had struck any vital organs.

There were thin clouds scudding across the face of the moon now, and Wilson's face was a pallid gray in the intermittent light. Storey could see the slight rise and fall of the sheriff's chest.

"Didn't get 'em, did I?" he said as Storey rode up.

"I don't believe so," The Boozer told him. He looked up at Storey. "Did he.?"

"No," Storey said. "They got away."

The Boozer didn't say anything, but it was obvious that he was wondering why Storey had not fired on them.

Storey wondered too. He simply hadn't been able to do it. Even the preacher had been able to shoot, but not Storey.

To add further to Storey's humiliation, The Boozer seemed to have regained a measure of his own confidence. He was examining Wilson's wounds as best he could under the circumstances, his hands moving with an assurance that Storey had never before seen in them.

The Reverend Stump had gotten out of his wagon, and his wife was clinging to him.

"Oh, Lawton," she said. "I didn't know that you were so brave."

Stump, for his part, looked a bit amazed himself. He looked down at the gun in his hand and put it in his buggy. His wife was clutching him too closely to allow him to stick it back into his belt.

"Oh, Lawton," Naomi said as the thought struck her. "I got the money. I got all the money."

"What money?" Stump said.

"All the money those men took," Naomi said, holding up the

flour sack. "Well, nearly all. They got sixty-three dollars at the medicine show. I expect they still have that."

She looked over at Storey as if to apologize for not having retrieved that money as well, but all Storey could think of was that even a woman was a better man than he was. She had gotten away from Sam and Ben Hawkins, and she had taken their money while he had again done nothing.

Naomi then glanced over to where The Boozer was treating Wilson. "There's something else," she said.

"Absolutely correct," The Boozer said. "We need to get this man to a doctor. I'm not sure I can get the bleeding stopped completely, and we need to get the bullet out of his side. There may be one in his shoulder as well."

"And where might we find a doctor?" Stump said.

Storey thought they might find one in New York City, but he didn't say so. He had lost any inclination he might ever have had to make smart remarks.

"There is no doctor in town," Stump went on. "Just a woman who sometimes serves as a midwife. She does do a bit of doctoring, but not for anything serious. Mostly colds and the like. The sort of thing your Indian Miracle Oil would work just as well for."

"You're a doctor," Storey said to The Boozer.

"I was once. Not now," The Boozer said.

"There's no one else," Stump said. "If you were a doctor at one time, you can't have forgotten everything."

The Boozer did not look happy about the situation. "I don't know."

Storey looked at Stuartson's hands. They had started shaking again.

"You've still got your medical bag," he said. "I've seen it in the wagon."

"A medical bag doesn't mean a thing," The Boozer said. "Anyone can buy one."

"Your instruments are in it. I know you've taken care of them."

The Boozer nodded. It was true that he still had enough pride to make sure that his instruments remained polished and sharp. He checked them fairly often.

"All right, then," Storey said, as if everything were settled. "We can borrow the preacher's buggy; we'll take the sheriff back to the wagon. You can get your bag and work on him there."

"I don't know," The Boozer said. "I'm not sure—"

"You're the only chance I've got," Wilson said, surprising them all. "You can't just let me get infected and die."

"He's right," Stump said. "You have to do what you can."

"It might not be enough." The Boozer said.

"It'll have to do," Storey said. "Let's see if we can get him in the buggy."

Naomi watched and listened to all this without trying to finish what she had been about to say. The men had thought she was talking about the sheriff, and she was, but she hadn't been thinking about his wounds.

Nevertheless, getting help for him was what really mattered now, not what she had overheard. She could tell them about that later.

Stump and Storey loaded Wilson into the back seat of the buggy, lifting him as carefully as they could. He moaned with pain as they let him down.

The Boozer stood by, watching gloomily. He was not at all sure he could do anything for the sheriff. In fact, he was afraid that he might be as likely to do him ill as to do him good. It had been a long time since he had tried any kind of surgery at all, even something as simple as removing a bullet, and that was a job that was not always as simple as it seemed.

He realized with a pang of disappointment that he was actually worried more about himself than he was about the wounded man. The Boozer had sunk to a low point, but there were still depths below him. If the sheriff died as a result of The Boozer's ministrations, those depths might open.

Where they might lead, The Boozer did not know, nor did he want to find out.

"Now then," Storey said when they had the sheriff safely stowed. "Let's get him back to the show wagon. That is, if you don't mind taking him, Preacher."

"I don't mind," Stump said. "It's the Lord's work." He helped Naomi into the front seat and climbed in beside her.

"Don't drive too fast," Storey said. "You don't want to bounce him around."

"You may set the pace," Stump said.

As they left the yard of the shack, Naomi watched the broad back of the tall young man in buckskins. Earlier she had wondered how it might feel to be crushed in his arms, but now she no longer even cared. It was her own husband who had come to her rescue at the last, gun blazing. She snuggled close to him, holding tight to his left arm, and she hoped the Vitality Pills hadn't been damaged when she hit Ben in the head with her purse. She was certain now that she was going to use them later, one way or another.

As for himself, the Reverend Stump was a bit confused. He was a man of peace, not a man of violence. He believed in the Lamb of God and the peace which passeth understanding, not in gunpowder.

But when prayer had not availed him, gunpowder had. He had not actually shot anyone, of course, but he had tried, and the feeling of potency the pistol had given him was almost intoxicating. He would have reached to touch its handle had not Naomi been clasping his arm.

He felt the nearness of her, the heat of her body as she pressed against him, and he was not repelled. On the contrary, he found himself enjoying very much the softness of her cheek as it rested on his shoulder, the even more tender softness of her breast as it flattened against him.

He thought of what it might be like to hold her to him, to press her to his breast and kiss her.

The thought was good, and for some reason no guilt accompanied it. For the life of him, he could not quite figure out why.

Those who lived by the sword died by the sword, he knew that, and he knew that the saying was just as true for the gun as for the sword. Knowing it, however, did not affect the way he felt, not a bit.

For the first time in his life, Lawton Stump began to wonder if the things that he had always preached were true.

/ Carl Gary had sent the town's undertaker, Tal Thurman, to the medicine show for the bodies, and Thurman was surprised to find that there was only one.

Barclay Sanders took advantage of the opportunity to hitch a ride back to town, since his own horse was nowhere to be found, having no doubt vanished during the shooting skirmish.

After they had loaded the dead man in the back of Thurman's wagon and covered him with a tarpaulin, the Colonel asked Sanders where Ray Storey was.

Sanders was sitting on the seat of the wagon. He looked down at the Colonel, who was standing nearby. "You mean the man who was watchin' me?"

"That's the one," the Colonel acknowledged.

"I thought his name was supposed to be Kit Carson."

"That is his stage name," the Colonel explained. "Ray Storey is his baptismal name."

"Oh," Sanders said. "Well, I don't know where he went. He went out of the tent to get you, I guess, and he never did come back. The next person to show up was you, and I didn't see him again."

"It doesn't matter," the Colonel said, thinking that perhaps Storey had gone to see about Dr. Stuartson. "I'll find him later. If your head begins to hurt you again after you return home, you needn't hesitate to take several doses of the Miracle Oil."

"I'll do that," Sanders said, who had already taken a couple of hefty swallows at the Colonel's instigation. "It's mighty tasty stuff, all right."

"And good for many ailments," the Colonel said. "Including nausea, catarrh,—"

"Never mind all that," Thurman said, speaking for the first time. He was a heavyset man with thick black eyebrows and looked more like a blacksmith than an undertaker. "I got to get this dead fella on back into town."

"Of course," the Colonel said. "I did not mean to delay you. I hope you will be at our show tomorrow night. And you, too, Mr. Sanders."

"You mean you're gonna give another show after gettin' shot up and robbed by the Hawkins brothers already?" Thurman said.

"Naturally," the Colonel said. "That was our original plan, and we will not be intimidated by any such display of wild hooliganism."

"Then you got less sense than I thought you had," Thurman said. He clucked his tongue and slapped the reins against the neck of his team.

The Colonel watched the wagon roll away for a moment and then started to the trees. He thought that Dr. Stuartson might be there with the mules. The doctor seemed to prefer the company of the animals to that of human beings most of the time, and the Colonel wasn't sure he blamed him.

But neither Storey nor Stuartson was with the mules, and in fact one of the beasts was missing. So was Storey's horse.

Wondering what was going on, the Colonel turned back to the wagon.

Louisa was standing at the rear of the wagon when he got there.

"Did Mr. Storey mention going anywhere when he spoke to you?" the Colonel said.

"No. Why, is he gone?" Louisa's tone implied that she did not care much one way or the other.

"He appears to have departed, and Dr. Stuartson with him."

"Where do you suppose they could have gone?" Sophia said, sticking her head out the back of the wagon.

"Maybe they went to rescue that woman," Louisa said, her eyes brightening in the moonlight. She hoped that she was right. If she was, then much of her faith in Ray Storey would be restored.

"Perhaps we are about to find out," the Colonel said. "There are riders coming."

Sophia climbed down from the wagon, and they all looked off down the road to where the advancing figures could be seen as dark silhouettes against the night sky.

The figures grew larger, and Louisa said, "It's Ray and Dr. Stuartson. But someone's with them."

So it is "Ray" again, is it, the Colonel thought.

"I wonder who's in the buggy," Sophia said.

It did not take long for them to find out. When the buggy arrived, Stump introduced himself and Naomi, and Storey explained that the sheriff had been wounded in a gunfight.

"There's no doctor in this town," he said. "The Boo—Dr. Stuartson's going to look after him."

"We can put him in the tent," Stuartson said, dismounting from the mule and handing the reins to Storey. "He has a bullet in his side, and possibly one in his shoulder. I need to examine him more closely."

"Do you think that you—?" the Colonel cut himself short and changed tacks. "Drive the buggy over to the tent, Mr. Stump. We can unload the sheriff there."

Stuartson knew what the Colonel had been about to say, but he took no offense. He had the same doubts himself. While the others followed the buggy to the tent, he stepped into the wagon for his medical bag.

It was in a cabinet on one side of the wagon, along with the rest of the doctor's meager worldly goods: a pair of doctor's saddlebags; another suit of clothes, somewhat shabby; and a daguerreotype of his former wife.

He looked at the picture for a moment, thinking that it did nothing to reveal the chestnut color of his wife's hair, the green of her eyes. He felt a familiar warmth as a powerful surge of self-pity flowed over him.

If only his wife had not left him. If only she had stood by him in his need. If only—

Tears stung his eyes as he held the picture and stared into the unseeing eyes of the woman he still loved. He set it back in the cabinet and looked around for something to drink.

Louisa watched as Storey and her father gently lowered the

wounded sheriff onto the bench under the lantern. She noted the way the buckskin shirt strained across Storey's back as his muscles worked.

"What about the man who robbed us?" the Colonel said when Wilson was lying safely on his back. "Did they do this?"

"They certainly did," Naomi said. "And they kidnapped me, as well."

"But you were rescued," Louisa said. "Was it the sheriff who saved you?"

Naomi looked down at Wilson, whose eyes were screwed shut with pain. "He came to do it," she said. "But the Hawkins brothers shot him."

"But you *were* rescued," Louisa insisted.

"Yes," Naomi said. She turned her eyes to Stump. "My husband came to save me. He was wonderful, firing his pistol at those men and never flinching when they fired back."

Stump stood a bit straighter and pulled in his stomach as much as he could. Louisa noticed the pistol that was stuck in his belt.

"But what about you, Mr. Storey?" Louisa said. "Weren't you there?"

"I was there," Storey admitted, not meeting her eyes.

"And those two men? Did you kill them?"

Stump naturally thought that the question was addressed to him, since he had been the only one doing any shooting.

"No," he said. "I did not kill them, though I have to confess that I tried. Since I am a minister of the gospel, perhaps it is just as well that my marksmanship is not nearly so skilful as Mr. Carson demonstrated his to be at your show this afternoon."

"And he didn't kill them, either," Louisa said.

"Why, no, he didn't," Stump said, somewhat surprised, now that he thought about it.

"Oh, he probably hadn't reloaded his pistol," Louisa said, but her words missed their target.

Storey had already left the tent.

Chapter Thirteen

Sam Hawkins reined Wilson's winded horse to a stop at a clearing and stood in the stirrups, looking back over his shoulder to see if he was being followed.

He did not like the sensation that he had experienced at the shack as the bullets were flying around him, the sick feeling that he might die at any moment. The fact was that he did not like for his life to be in jeopardy. He might have a pretty miserable existence, but he had no wish to exchange it for no existence at all.

He had spent a good deal of his life engaged in dangerous pursuits, and he had been shot at more times than that one, but he had always taken care to eliminate as many of the risks as he could. He always liked to have the element of surprise on his own side, the way it had been in his and Ben's sudden ride on the medicine show or in their unexpected attack on Wilson.

In cases like that, Sam had learned, there was really very little chance that he would be the one who got hurt. By the time the victims figured out what was going on, Sam was usually in control of things, one way or the other.

Only a couple of times had things worked out the wrong way. One of them had been the time Wilson rode down the kid who ran into the street after the bank robbery. Some idiot in the bank had decided to be a hero, and after that it seemed like the whole town had come running. He and Ben had been damn lucky to get away that time.

And then tonight. Who would ever have thought that the preacher would come riding in like that, blasting at them like he was some damn gunfighter? It had been a surprise, all right, and Sam didn't like surprises.

And then that other bastard in the fancy outfit had tried to ride him down. Didn't draw his guns, though, just like he didn't at the medicine show, which was just as well as far as Sam was concerned. If he'd been shooting too, Sam might not have gotten away without a few bullet holes punched through his skin.

And speaking of bullet holes, Sam wondered if Ben had escaped. It had been a lucky thing for Sam that Wilson's horse was standing there and hadn't tried to take off on him, but Ben hadn't had that advantage.

Sam settled back down on his saddle and listened for any sounds of pursuit. Hearing nothing of that nature, he decided that he might as well wait for a while. Maybe Ben would show up, and now that Sam was ready, he wouldn't mind if that buckskin-wearing dude came along. Sam was always ready to take on a man who was afraid to draw.

There was a deadfall near the clearing. A tall pine had been struck by lightning about three-quarters of the way down its trunk, and the top had fallen to the ground, dragging several smaller trees with it.

Sam rode behind the deadfall and waited, his pistol drawn and cocked. He was good at waiting.

The moon was going down now, but it was still quite bright, and it threw long, dark shadows into the clearing. A faint breeze rustled the tops of the pines, and back in the trees a raccoon skittered across the pine needles. Sam hardly noticed these things. He concentrated on watching the clearing through the branches of the fallen trees.

In a few minutes, there was a louder noise than a small animal like a raccoon could make, that of a horse running as fast as it could through the thick growth.

There was another noise, too, the sound of a man yelling.

"Stop, goddammit! Stop right now, you lop-eared son of a bitch!"

Sam recognized Ben's voice, eased his pistol off the cock, and slid it into its holster.

Just then, Ben's horse hurtled into the clearing, Ben hanging onto its neck for dear life.

Sam rode out from behind the deadfall, and Ben's horse, as if finally deciding to obey his shouted commands, planted its front feet solidly, coming to a dead stop.

Ben, however, did not stop. He kept right on going, sailing ass over elbows out into the middle of the clearing, where he landed in a sprawl, his face buried in pine needles.

He sat up and looked around, feeling himself to see if he was all in one piece. His face, what could be seen of it, was scratched where tree branches had lashed him, or where the cat had scratched him, and one eye was tearing, but otherwise he seemed to be all right.

He saw Sam sitting on the sheriff's horse and looked at his brother reproachfully.

"You could've waited and let me ride double," he said. "I didn't have time to saddle up, and that damn fence-crawler there ain't used to being rode without a saddle. Damn near like to have killed me."

He stood up and brushed himself off, wincing as he hit a bruise.

"You shouldn't ought to run off and leave your brother like that, Sam," he said. "Even if you didn't want to ride double, you coulda waited for me."

"You got away, didn't you?" Sam said. "Don't whine so much."

"I ain't whinin'. I just don't think—"

"Never mind what you think. What happened back there? Did you shoot any of 'em?"

"Hell, I don't think so. It was all I could do to get away before somebody shot me. I didn't stick around to count any bodies."

"It was that preacher that came in shootin', wasn't it?" Sam said. "The same one who preached about us in his church that time?"

"It sure looked like him," Ben agreed. "And one of them others was from the medicine show. The one in that fancy outfit. I didn't know that other one, the one on the mule."

"He was probably from that medicine show, too," Sam said, and then he remembered the worst thing of all. "And that bitch took all our money."

"All of it?" Ben said.

"All but that piddlin' sixty-three dollars. I've still got that much. But we had nearly two thousand dollars in that flour sack."

"I knew we shoulda found a better place for it," Ben said. "I told you more than once—"

"Shut up," Sam said. He was thinking. There had to be something they could do about the money. And he didn't like being shot at, either. Somebody was going to have to pay for that in a way that would give Sam the upper hand.

"What're we gonna do, Sam?" Ben said.

"We're gonna get our money back," Sam said. "And we're gonna make that preacher sorry he was ever born."

"What about his wife?"

"Her too," Sam said. "Her too."

Storey found Stuartson in the show wagon with a bottle of Miracle Oil in his hand. The bottle was two-thirds empty, and Stuartson was about to slug down the rest of its contents when Storey grabbed his wrist and jerked the bottle away from his mouth.

Stuartson dropped the bottle, and the Miracle Oil splashed on his medical bag and trickled onto the floor. The Boozer watched sadly as it soaked into the boards.

"You ought to be ashamed of yourself," Storey said.

"I needed it," Stuartson said. "Look at my hands." He held them up for Storey to see the trembling.

"They weren't shaking when you looked that sheriff over a while ago," Storey said. "I think that's just an excuse."

The Boozer looked at him shrewdly. "You're very astute when it comes to analyzing the failures of others."

"Never mind about that," Storey said, his face reddening. "You pick up that bag and come on. They're waiting for you in the tent."

Stuartson bent down and took his bag by the handle. "Don't make me do this," he said as he straightened.

"If there was anybody else who could do it, I wouldn't. But you're all we got."

Stuartson looked at him pleadingly. "But what if he dies? What if I can't save him?"

"What difference does that make?" Storey said. "He's going to die if you *don't* help him, isn't he? This way, at least he's got some kind of a chance."

"I never thought of things in exactly that way," Stuartson said.

"Well, it's time you started," Storey told him. "Now come on." He took Stuartson's arm and pulled him to the rear of the wagon.

"We need alcohol," Stuartson said. "For antiseptic. And something for bandages."

Storey located a bottle and a few yards of material that Sophia Mahaffey had been saving to make a new dress with. He picked it up.

"This ought to do," he said. "What else?"

"That will serve," Stuartson said. "I'm ready now."

"Good. Let's go."

"Ah, there you are," the Colonel said as they stepped outside. "The sheriff is in a great deal of pain."

"Dr. Stuartson will get the bullets out now," Storey said. "He was looking for his bag."

When they got inside the tent, Wilson was unconscious. The pain had been too great, and he had passed out.

"Probably for the best," Stuartson said. "I'll need the men to stay here and hold him. The women might want to go inside the wagon."

The women did not want to go. "We might be able to be of some help," Sophia said, speaking for all of them.

"Very well," Stuartson said, taking off his coat and rolling up his sleeves. "If you'll pour a little of that alcohol on my hands, Mr. Storey, I'll begin."

Storey poured the alcohol while Stuartson rubbed his hands together. They had stopped shaking.

Sam and Ben rode back to their house. They figured that they would be as safe there as anywhere.

"The way we were runnin', they'll think we're in Kansas by now," was the way Ben put it.

Sam knew Ben was right, but he didn't like to hear the part about running.

"We weren't runnin'," he said. "Just tryin' to keep from gettin' killed."

Ben couldn't quite see the difference, but he didn't say anything. Sam had always been smarter than he was.

The cat was sleeping on the porch when they rode up, but he jumped off and ran under the house when the horses came into the yard. Sam's usual mount was still in the lean-to.

"How about Coy's horse?" Ben said. "We gonna keep him?"

"Might as well," Sam said, looking around the yard. "Looks like they carted Coy off, though."

"We didn't have any use for him, now did we?" Sam said.

They put up the horses and went to the house. Sam lit a lamp that sat in the middle of the table, and they sat in the two chairs.

"You decided yet what we're gonna do?" Ben said. He didn't bother trying to make any plans of his own. Sam was always the one with the plans.

"Yeah," Sam said. "We're gonna check out that medicine show tomorrow. If they stay in town, we'll wait till ever'body goes out to see the show and then we'll ride into town and kick the damn place apart. If anybody's there and gets in our way, that's just too bad."

"What about the buryin'?" Ben said. "Won't that be tomorrow? Maybe we could go then."

It wasn't a bad idea, but Sam didn't pay any attention to it since he hadn't thought of it.

"We'll wait. It'll be better to go in later. That way, it'll be dark if they try to chase after us. Besides, after we finish in town, I want us to go out to that show and kick them apart, too."

That sounded fine to Ben. "What about that woman?" he said. "She threw that damn cat on me. I'd like to whip her for doin' that."

"We won't have time for foolin' with women, this time," Sam said. "We won't be stickin' around. I think old Coy was right about one thing. It's time we were gettin' ourselves back up to Kansas. After this, I think Texas might get a little too warm for us."

"What'll we do for money?" Ben said.

"I'll think of somethin'," Sam said.

Ben nodded. Sam would think of something, all right. He always did.

Sweat was rolling off Dr. Stuartson's forehead, and Sophia Mahaffey blotted it with a piece of cloth. The lantern light made the tent glow.

The Colonel and Ray Storey were holding Coy Wilson's arms while Stuartson worked on him. Lawton, Naomi, and Louisa stood off to one side, watching quietly. There was a strong smell of alcohol and blood in the air.

As far as Stuartson could tell, there was no bullet in Wilson's shoulder. The lead had passed through cleanly. But there was no exit wound in the sheriff's side. Stuartson believed that the bullet had struck a rib and been deflected downward. However, although he had made an incision near where he thought the bullet should be, he had not as yet been able to locate it.

No one spoke as Stuartson probed for the bullet with steady hands.

Occasionally the sheriff's body gave a severe twitch, but the Colonel and Storey had a firm grip. Wilson hardly moved on the bench.

Stuartson bit his lip in concentration. He was barely conscious of the sweat that threatened to drip into his eyes before Sophia wiped it off. His only concern was to find the bullet.

What if I'm wrong? he thought. It was certainly possible. The bullet could be anywhere. It could have deflected upward, or it could have gone straight into the back muscles and not been deflected at all. The trouble was that Stuartson couldn't afford to be wrong. He couldn't simply continue to cut on the sheriff, looking for the bullet first in one place and then in another. The sheriff would bleed to death before Stuartson ever found a thing. He had to be right the first time.

Stuartson closed his eyes as Sophia wiped his brow again. He was suddenly convinced that he had made a fatal error. He would never find the bullet he was looking for, and the sheriff would surely die.

What difference does that make? Stuartson asked himself. *You didn't shoot the man.*

It was no good to tell himself things like that, however. Knowing that he had not shot Wilson made no real difference. If the sheriff died, Stuartson would take the blame for the death upon himself.

"How you doin', Doc?" Storey said.

Stuartson spared him a glance, and Storey said, "Remember what I told you."

"What was that?" the Colonel said.

"Nothing much," Storey said, knowing that Stuartson remembered, all right.

Stuartson knew that Storey had been right, up to a point. If Stuartson didn't get the bullet out, the sheriff would die even more surely than if Stuartson made a mistake, but the fact that the bullet was there was not Stuartson's doing. Stuartson wasn't solely responsible for the man's life. The men who shot him had made sure of that. Stuartson was merely being given an opportunity to undo some of the harm that others had done. If he succeeded, that was fine; if he failed, then others were much more to blame for the death than Stuartson was.

The same thing could be said to be true of any death that occurred under a doctor's care, Stuartson supposed, as long as the doctor did his utmost to ensure the patient's survival. If the doctor made no mistakes, did the very best that he knew how, then there was no need for him to carry the guilt for the patient's death.

But what if the doctor *did* make a mistake, as Stuartson was becoming increasingly sure he had done now? What if—

Stuartson's probe encountered the bullet. He had been right after all. His knees threatened to give way under him as the relief flooded through him. He took a deep breath and let it out slowly.

He put the probe down and took a forceps. It was only a matter of seconds before he had removed the bullet. Then he cleansed the wound and closed it, along with the shoulder wound. It seemed to Stuartson that the sheriff was already breathing easier.

"Congratulations, Doctor," the Colonel said, extending a bloody hand, which Stuartson took in his own, even more gory. "You did a superb job."

"Sure did," Storey said. "I knew he had it in him."

"We all did," Louisa said.

I didn't, Stuartson thought as he accepted their congratulations. He badly needed a drink, and he needed it soon.

Chapter Fourteen

"There's something I think everyone should know," Naomi said, interrupting the acclamation for Doctor Stuartson, who took the opportunity to slip out unnoticed.

Everyone turned to her. "What is it, Naomi?" her husband said.

"It's something I overheard the Hawkins brothers saying," she told them. "Something about the sheriff."

"What about him?" the Colonel said.

Naomi told them as much as she could remember of what she had heard.

"And do you mean to say that he not only knew of their villainy but participated in it?" the Colonel said when she was finished.

"I'm certain that's true," Naomi said. "But he seemed sorry for having done it. He wanted them to go away and leave the town alone now. He seemed to know that he had been wrong."

"The Bible tells us that a man can be born again," the Reverend Stump said.

"But those men appear to have been bleeding the town white," Louisa said. "And with the help of their chosen officer."

"Yes," Naomi said. "And think of what they did to the church when you spoke against them, Lawton. The sheriff refused to do a thing."

"The Bible also tells us to be forgiving, to turn the other cheek," Stump said, trying to sound convinced. At the same time, he felt his fingers straying to the butt of the pistol in his belt, and he had to force his hand away.

"There's one other thing," Naomi said. "I think they blamed the sheriff for running someone down, maybe killing him. A 'kid,' they said. It happened in Kansas." She recounted what she had heard of that part of the story.

"We must not be too hasty to judge," the Colonel said. "It may be that you misunderstood. We'll have to ask the sheriff about these things when he recovers."

Storey was aghast at this last revelation, however, and had no desire to ask the sheriff about it. His entire body was drenched in a cold sweat as he thought about how he had been deceived for so long and about how the very man who was actually responsible for Chet's death was lying unconscious right there in the tent.

It had not been Sam Hawkins who had ridden over Chet. Storey had only assumed that because he had learned Sam's name. He could have fixed on Ben just as easily and been just as wrong. It had been the third man, the one whose name Storey had learned only now, just after having encouraged Stuartson to save the man's life.

Storey's own hands were shaking now as much as Stuartson's had been earlier, and he pressed them into the sides of his legs so that no one would notice. His mind whirled in confusion. He needed to get out of the tent, to go somewhere and think things over.

While the others continued to talk, he slipped out of the tent and went into the trees. His horse was there, still saddled. Louisa had taken the horse there, along with Sunny, but she had not taken care of the gear.

Storey uncinched the girth and slid off the saddle. Then he took the reins and led the horse down to the spring for a drink. Storey knelt down beside the horse, dipped his hands in the water, and splashed his face with the cool liquid.

He sat back in the grass and looked up at the sky and the lowering moon. He could feel the skin of his face tighten as the water dried.

His thoughts were confused and angry. For a year now he had been looking for a man, wanting to kill him. When he'd finally found the man, he hadn't been able even to draw his gun on him, though the desire to kill him was just as strong as ever.

And now he'd found out that the man he'd been wanting to kill wasn't the right man after all. The man who had caused Chet's suffering and death was lying back there in the medicine show tent, nearly dead himself, and Storey had not had a hand in things at all.

It just didn't seem right to Storey. There was something wrong with all of it, some essential failure of justice.

The horse was through drinking, and Storey stood up and led it back to where the mules waited, where he hobbled it. He removed the bridle and then took Sunny down to drink. When Sunny was through, Storey took off the hackamore. The mules didn't need hobbling. They never seemed to wander off.

"You take good care of those animals," Louisa said.

Storey turned around and saw her standing there. There were shadows on her face, but he thought she might be smiling.

"I like horses and mules," he said. He didn't know what else to say. His hands felt unexpectedly large and clumsy, and he didn't know what to do with them.

"I saw you leave the tent," Louisa said. "You looked upset."

"I guess I was, a little bit," he said. "Can't stand the sight of blood."

"That wasn't it." Louisa walked over to where he was standing. "It was something else, something that Mrs. Stump said."

Storey had never told anyone about his brother. He believed that a man kept things like that to himself, and he had not wanted to explain to the Colonel that his only reason for joining the show was to hunt for a man he wanted to kill.

"It was when she told about that child that the sheriff ran down," Louisa said. "I saw your face."

Storey had thought of Louisa as a very pretty young woman, when he allowed her to intrude on his thoughts at all, but he had never before realized how observant she was.

"That kid was my brother," he said.

"Your brother! How awful!" Louisa's eyes were shining with tears.

Storey decided that he might as well tell her the whole thing, so he did.

"And you were going to kill the man responsible?" she said when he was finished. There were no tears in her eyes now. "I don't blame you."

"But I didn't," Storey said. "I didn't do anything."

"You would have been killing the wrong man if you had."

"They were all a part of it. And that doesn't make any difference anyway. I thought Sam Hawkins was the right man, and I should have done something about it, for my brother's sake."

"Your brother doesn't care," said a voice from the opposite side of the tree where Storey and Louisa were standing.

Dr. Stuartson came out around the tree trunk where he had been standing. He was holding a half-empty bottle of Miracle Oil in his right hand.

"Forgive me for having listened to your conversation," he said. "I just happened to be where I could not avoid hearing you."

"You're not supposed to have that," Louisa said, with an accusatory look at the bottle Stuartson was holding. "Father will be very disappointed."

"We don't have to tell him," Stuartson pointed out. He held up the bottle and looked to see how much Miracle Oil was left inside. "I think I deserved it, to tell the truth."

"You did save that man's life," Louisa admitted.

"Maybe," Stuartson said. "And now Mr. Storey is wondering if it was even worth saving."

"The man killed my brother," Storey said.

"And how do you feel about that?" Stuartson said. "Outraged? Or is it just a kind of sadness?"

Storey realized for the first time that he really no longer felt the same way he had when his travels had begun. Then the desire to kill Sam Hawkins had burned in his gut like a prairie fire, but now there was nothing more than a dull ache there in the spot. And even the fact of Chet's death did not hurt him the way that it once had.

"How did you know?" Storey said.

"I am a man of some experience when it comes to sadness and regret," Stuartson said. He put the bottle to his mouth, tilted it, and took a swallow of the Miracle Oil. "I simply found a different way of dealing with those things than you did."

"You mean drinking," Louisa said. "I wish you'd give me that bottle."

"Not until I'm finished," Stuartson said. "Allow me to explain what I mean."

"There's no need for that," Storey said. He wasn't interested in what Stuartson had to say. What could The Boozer know about how Storey felt?

"I believe there is a need," Stuartson said. "I think our stories might be similar in some ways."

Storey shook his head. "I don't see how."

"That's what I'm going to tell you. I never wanted to kill anyone, of course, but I did have a deep pain that I had to somehow learn to deal with. I should have faced it, but I found a simpler way. I lost everything of value I ever had, but I didn't have to face my pain."

"And you think I'm like that?" Storey said.

"Oh, no," Stuartson said. "Quite the contrary. You have accepted your pain and sought to face your demons. It's just that when you faced them—"

"They got the best of me," Storey said.

"No, no. Mine got the best of me." Stuartson took another drink from the bottle. "As I discovered. You seem to have discovered something else."

"And you're going to tell me what that is?"

"That is correct. You've discovered that you're not a natural killer."

"You make it sound almost like a good thing," Storey said. "But some people don't see it that way."

Louisa put a hand on his arm. "I do. Now."

Storey wished that he could believe them. He certainly wanted to. But it wasn't easy. It seemed like there should be a difference between killing because it came natural to you, like it did for Sam and Ben, and killing because it was an obligation.

Besides, there was more to what had happened than that.

"I should have defended us this evening," Storey said. "I didn't even do that."

"Suppose you had," Stuartson said. "Suppose you had drawn your pistol and opened fire—"

"It wasn't loaded," Louisa pointed out.

"Even if it had been. Those two men had their guns already in their hands. They would most likely have killed you and the others. What good would that have done?"

Storey knew the answer to that. He would have died thinking that he was a brave man instead of a coward.

He said as much.

Stuartson took the last swallow of the Miracle Oil and put the bottle in his back pocket.

"You'd still be dead," he said "And so would Miss Mahaffey here, undoubtedly. Look at what you did do. You went after the men didn't you?"

"When it was almost too late. And I didn't shoot then, either."

"You rode at that man in the face of gunfire," Stuartson said. "That showed courage."

Louisa agreed, but Storey was still not convinced. "I should have done more," he said.

"The secret is to know when the time has really come to use a gun," Stuartson said. "That's the real test."

"When's that time?" Storey said.

"When you can't do anything else." Stuartson looked through the trees at the sinking moon. "But why listen to me? I'm simply an old drunk who follows a medicine show."

"You're a little more than that," Storey said. "After tonight, anyway."

Stuartson patted his pocket. "Only a little more. But I have a patient to look after, if you'll excuse me." He left them and walked in the direction of the tent.

Storey watched him go. "Do you think he's right?" he said.

Louisa wasn't sure that she understood everything Stuartson had said. She thought that she would have been happier if Storey had drawn his guns. That was what a man was supposed to do. Lawton Stump had done it, and he was a preacher. But she would not have wanted Ray to be like one of the Hawkins brothers, or even like the sheriff, if it was true that he had ridden over Ray's brother and killed him.

She had believed she had her thoughts all straightened out, and now she found that she was more confused than ever.

"I hope he's right," she said finally. It was the best she could do, though it was not exactly what Storey had hoped to hear.

The Stumps went back to town in the buggy, leaving the sheriff behind. Stuartson had agreed to look after him through the night.

"I don't need the sleep," The Boozer said. "I get plenty of that during the day."

The Stumps agreed to keep the sheriff's involvement with the Hawkins brothers a secret. They would let him tell about it when he recovered, if he saw fit to do so.

They also agreed that they would begin returning the townspeople's money to them as soon as possible the next day. It might not be easy to determine exactly how much was owed to each one, but something could surely be worked out. They knew that everyone would be thrilled to know that the Hawkinses had been put to rout and the money recovered.

Finally, they had decided to return to the medicine show the next afternoon.

"It will be even better," the Colonel promised. "I can assure you of that. Why, we did not even have time for the anatomy lecture, one of the most educational and enlightening parts of the entire show."

"I won't be able to attend that part, however," Naomi said.

"True, true. But I'm sure your husband will find it quite educational, and Dr. Stuartson is well qualified to lecture on the muscular structure of the body, as you have learned here tonight."

Naomi did not mind being excluded. What she wanted to do was get home and try the Indian Vitality Pills on her husband, but from the attention he was showing her, she somehow felt that she might not even need them.

When the Stumps had departed, Sophia drew her husband aside to talk.

"I believe more than ever that we should leave here," she said. "I don't think that it would be wise to do another show."

"And why is that?" the Colonel said, still feeling the enthusiasm that had come over him when he was discussing the anatomy lecture with the Stumps, the same enthusiasm that always came over him when he was talking about the show, no matter how many times he did it.

"I wish I knew. It may be that I've been pretending to be Ro-Shanna for so long that I'm beginning to believe in Indian magic."

The Colonel laughed and drew her to him. "You heard what Mr. Stump said. The heathen Hawkins brothers have taken to their heels and fled the country. We are not likely to be bothered by them any further."

She yielded to his embrace, but she felt no easier in her mind about the coming show. She wished that there was some way to convince him, but she supposed there wasn't.

She had been right the first time, however. And she was afraid that she was going to be right again.

Chapter Fifteen

The next morning came clear and hot, with the sun burning through a few low clouds and flaming in the blue sky.

Sam and Ben were up early, planning to do their best to make sure that Sophia's premonition became a reality.

They were sitting on their porch, drinking Arbuckle's coffee out of dented tin cups. There was a small fire beside the house where Sam had boiled the coffee.

Ben put down his cup and checked the loads in his pistol. He rolled the cylinder against the heel of his hand.

"Wonder where that damn cat is," he said, sighting down his pistol barrel at a pine cone that lay in the yard. "I'd like to do a little something to him, sort of pay him back for a few of these scratches on my face."

"Save your ammunition," Sam said. He hadn't seen the cat that morning, either. "You're going to need it later on, when we take care of that town."

"Those townies are in for a real surprise," Ben said, forgetting the cat and thinking about how much fun he was going to have getting back at everyone else.

"Especially that preacher," Sam said. "I want to give him a small sample of what hell's like in the good old here and now. I'd like to blow him apart like I did that terrapin yesterday, send him spinnin' in the street with the top of that bald head split into as many pieces as that terrapin's shell."

Ben thought that was a fine idea, but he was sorry about one thing. "That wife of his is sure a fine-lookin' woman. I wish you could see your way clear to lettin' us have a little fun with her before we leave here. I was really lookin' forward to gettin' that dress off her." He scratched savagely at the beard under his chin. "Besides, she was the one threw the cat on me, and no woman oughta be allowed to get away with doin' a thing like that to a man."

"She was a prime piece, all right," Sam agreed. "Full of spunk, too. But we ain't got time for nothin' like that. We got to strike fast and move out. That's the best way."

As usual, Ben knew that Sam was right. But it still seemed like a damned shame to let a woman like that go to waste on a fat preacher. Sometimes it seemed like there was just no justice in the world.

Just at that moment, Naomi would not have agreed. As far as she was concerned, the world was fully just and completely wonderful.

Lawton had proved that to her last night.

She did not know how she had ever come to doubt him, or why she had felt compelled to buy those pills. They certainly hadn't needed them. Lawton had been a different man.

She turned over in their tangled bed and looked out the window at the sun.

It wasn't really fair to say that Lawton had been different. At the very beginning of their marriage he had been the way he was last night, but only at the beginning. Something had changed him then, and now something had changed him back.

She did not know what it was, but she knew that as long as he stayed that way she would never have to look at some tall stranger in buckskins and wonder how it would feel to be in his arms. She would be completely happy not knowing, just as long as she had Lawton.

The Reverend Stump was already in the church, kneeling at the altar. Everything should have been fine with him now, and he wondered why it was not. He was having no more luck in praying than he had experienced the day before.

Could it be the gun that was sticking in his belt?

He had never carried a gun into church before, and he had never allowed anyone else to do so, but here he was. He allowed his hand to stray to the handle, to move over the smooth wooden grips.

The gun had made him feel different, more powerful, taller, even slimmer and more handsome.

He knew the feeling was wrong, and he wondered if it was Satan's way of misleading him. He had studied the Bible for too long not to know that the way of violence really never solved anything.

He got up from the altar and went to the room that served as his office. There was a roll-top desk in there, with locking drawers.

He took the pistol from his belt and weighed it in his hand. The solid feel of it reminded him of the way it had bucked in his hand when he had shot at the Hawkins brothers, and he could remember the look of fear that had been in Sam Hawkins's eyes as he fled into the house.

Reluctantly, he opened the bottom drawer of the desk. There was nothing in it except for a few blank sheets of ledger paper. He laid the gun on the paper and closed the drawer. He looked through the pigeon holes on top of the desk until he found the drawer key, and locked the gun in. It wouldn't tempt him anymore.

His thoughts turned to Naomi.

She had responded to him last night as she never had before, and he realized that he had been a fool ever to have rejected her love. There was no sin in it, surely not as much sin as there was in the gun. The Lord had admonished his creatures to be fruitful and multiply, and nowhere could Stump remember having read that the act leading to that fruitfulness and multiplying should not bring pleasure.

The sin lay instead in letting the love of one's spouse, an earthly love, replace heavenly devotion and duty, and Stump knew now that he would never do that.

He would never let the gun replace those things, either. He had not been wrong to use it, he told himself, but he had been wrong to think that it would solve all his problems.

There was a time to use a gun, yes, he believed that. To all things there was a season. But there was also a time to lay the gun aside. He had done that now, and he would not pick it up again.

It had brought him what he had sought, his wife's forgiveness, or so it seemed.

Now he had to forgive himself.

He went back out to the altar. This time when he knelt, his prayer came easily.

Ray Storey rode into town early to remind everyone about the show, to pass out more handbills, and to inform the people about the condition of their sheriff.

He didn't intend to tell them everything about their sheriff, however. Everyone connected with the medicine show had agreed with the Stumps that some things were best not brought out into the open just yet.

Storey had not made up his own mind about how he felt, either. Wilson might be the sheriff, he might be wounded, and he might even have changed his relationship with the Hawkins brothers, but he was still the man who had killed Chet.

Storey told himself that he still had to do something about that. He just didn't know what.

Wilson had been much improved that morning, and he had wanted to return to town, but Dr. Stuartson had not recommended it.

"It would be best for you to rest and recuperate," Stuartson said. "Time enough for you to go into town tomorrow."

"But the Hawkins brothers," Wilson protested. "I have to do something about the Hawkins brothers."

"Never mind about them," Stuartson told him. "They were put to flight by an unlikely quartet." He told Wilson what had happened the night before after the sheriff had been shot.

"I'm not so sure that Sam and Ben would just take off like that," Wilson said. "I know those two better'n anybody." He didn't explain what he meant, but Stuartson knew.

"We don't need to discuss how well you know them," Stuartson said. "I can assure you that I saw them running, and the man who pursued them was not able to locate them."

That last part was not exactly true, as Stuartson was well aware, but he did not want to explain to Wilson that Storey's pursuit had been halfhearted at best.

"Besides," Stuartson went on, "you are in no condition to ride a horse, and we have no other method of conveyance here. You have lost a considerable amount of blood, and you have been weakened by your wounds. I suggest that you simply relax, rest, and wait until after this evening's show. Someone will surely be glad to give you a ride back into town."

As long as they don't know about your relationship to those two men, Stuartson thought, and he surely wasn't going to be the one to tell them. If the sheriff had somehow managed to break his ties with those two rapscallions, so much the better. Stuartson thought it was fine for someone to change his life; he wished he could change his own.

For a minute or two the previous evening, he even thought it might be possible, but of course it was not. He had sought out the bottle of Miracle Oil as soon as he got a chance, and he knew that within a few minutes he would be again sitting under a tree with another bottle in his hand. He was full of good advice for others, but overcoming his own problems was something else again.

One of the first people that Storey encountered when he rode into town was Carl Gary, who was strolling along the boardwalk outside the saloon.

Storey walked his horse over in that direction.

The saloon owner was surprised to see someone from the medicine show, and he was even more surprised when Storey gave him a handbill and asked him to come to the show that would be held that afternoon.

"You mean to tell me that there will be another show?" Gary said. "After what happened last night?"

"The Colonel thought folks would appreciate seeing it," Storey said. "After all, they didn't stick around to see all of it yesterday."

Gary thought that Storey might be trying to insult him, and he didn't like it. He didn't like the way Storey sat there on his horse and didn't get down and talk to him about matters face to face.

"Our lives were in danger," he said, looking up at Storey and brushing his thin moustache. "We had no way of protecting ourselves."

"I didn't mean to say you did," Storey told him. "I just meant that you missed the anatomy lecture, one of the best parts of the show. The Colonel hopes you'll all be back."

"Humph," Gary said. "No doubt he's hoping to get more of our money to replace what the Hawkins brothers took last night. And they may well be back to do the same tonight if there's another show."

"I don't think so," Storey said. "Haven't you heard about that?"

"About what?" Gary said. "I was just on my way to the jail to check on the sheriff. He rode out to their shack last night, but he didn't come by to tell me what he accomplished. Do you know?"

He looked at Storey suspiciously, wondering how someone from the medicine show could have found out more than one of the leading citizens of the town. He didn't like the idea of someone knowing more about things around town than he knew himself. It wasn't the way things ought to be.

"I know, all right," Storey said. "But it might be better if you heard it from your preacher. He's the one to tell it, since he was involved in it, and he has some good news for you and the rest of the folks in town."

"What kind of good news?"

"Like I said, you ought to hear it from him. Why don't you go over to his house and ask him? Take a few other folks with you. They're going to like what he has to say."

"All right, then," Gary said. He didn't like to be talked to in such a fashion, but it seemed that there was nothing more that Mr. Kit Carson, or whatever his real name might be, was going to tell him.

Storey rode his horse on down toward the church while Gary went around talking to the people on the street and in the stores. Before long a respectable crowd was on its way to the church.

Just as the first of them arrived, led by Gary, Lawton Stump emerged from the church door.

He seemed surprised to see everyone, and he looked at Storey inquiringly.

"I told them to come on over here," Storey said. "They hadn't heard any of the news."

"Oh," Stump said. "I see."

He was momentarily flustered by seeing such a gathering in front of his church, but he was naturally a good speaker, and it didn't take him long to regain his composure and begin telling the tale.

Everyone was amazed to hear about the kidnapping of Mrs. Stump. There was a great deal of muttering, especially among the men, about what should be done to the Hawkins brothers if they were ever seen again, even though most of those same men had done nothing to them before.

"Was she harmed?" a woman in the front asked.

"No," Stump said. "Thank God, we were in time."

He went on to tell how he, Storey, and Stuartson had all arrived at about the same time, putting the Hawkinses on the run, just after the shooting of Sheriff Wilson.

"You mean to tell us that the Hawkins brothers are run off?" Gary said. "And you're the one that did it?"

"That's what I mean," Stump said.

"And you say the sheriff's shot?" Gary said. "Did they kill him?"

"I believe they thought so," Stump said. "And he very well might have died if not for the skill of the doctor who travels with the medicine show. Stuartson is his name."

"I thought that most of those men were drunks, or worse," the woman who had asked about Naomi said.

"Some of them may be," Stump admitted. "But this one performed a delicate surgery to remove a bullet and save the sheriff's life."

"I guess he helped me, too," Barclay Sanders said, walking to the front of the group. He stood there with a clean bandage around his head, waiting to get a little of the attention. He had been too groggy to remember who had fixed him up the night before, but he was willing to assume that it had been Stuartson for the chance to get a ray or two of reflected glory.

Storey listened, smiling, thinking how much the Colonel would have enjoyed this. There wasn't a person there who wouldn't want to come to the show that night, just to see The Boozer.

"And where is the sheriff now?" Gary said.

"He's out at the show," Storey said. Everyone's eyes were turned to him. "Dr. Stuartson is taking care of him, dosing him with Miracle Oil, I might add. You can come this afternoon and see for yourselves how well he's doing."

People were nodding, smiling, shaking their heads. Storey would have to tell the Colonel to make up plenty of Miracle Oil to sell at the show. There would be a good number of eager customers.

"But there is still more good news," Stump said, and people turned back to hear him. "While Mrs. Stump was held prisoner in the Hawkins brothers' shack, she found a sack full of money—your money. And she recovered it."

The eagerness the crowd had displayed before was nothing to what they showed now.

It was Gary who expressed what most of them were thinking. "How much did she find? And where is it?"

146

"It is right inside my house," Stump said. "And I believe that there is nearly two thousand dollars."

People clapped their hands, whistled, cheered. This was better than the medicine show, and just at the right moment, Naomi Stump came out of her house holding a flour sack in front of her.

Storey watched her walk through the yard. *The Squaw Ro-Shanna could learn something about how to make entrances from her,* he thought.

"Here it is," she said, moving to stand beside her husband. "All I could find of it, anyway."

"We are going to return the money," Stump told them. "Just as soon as each of you can make a reckoning of how much was taken from you. If it is not all there, we will divide it proportionally."

He was afraid it would not all be there; he suspected that the sheriff had taken a share. But maybe that too could be recovered in a way that would not be damaging to the sheriff if the man had indeed renounced his unlawful companions.

"I can tell you to the penny how much they took from me," Gary said.

"Me, too," Sanders said. "To the very last damn penny." Realizing where he was, he added, "Excuse my language preacher. Ma'am."

No one seemed to mind. They were all caught up in the excitement of the moment.

When they had calmed down for a minute, Storey reminded them again that there would be another show that afternoon and that Dr. Stuartson would be conducting the anatomy lecture.

"Women and children not admitted, of course. But there will be a chance for everyone to see the doctor's skills as they were practiced on the terrible wounds suffered by Sheriff Wilson. The sheriff himself will be there to watch the show. The show begins an hour before sundown."

"I can vouch for the Miracle Oil, too," Sanders said. "It sure got me over the rough patches last night after those Hawkins boys shot me in the head and left me for dead."

People gathered around to look at Sander's head, but others wanted to know more about the money.

"Make out a reckoning," Stump repeated. "My wife and I will see that you get back at least the greater part of what is owed to you."

The group began to break up after that, with most of the women staying behind to commiserate with Naomi Stump about her ordeal, or to find out as many of the sordid details as she was willing to tell them.

Storey passed out as many handbills as he could, but he knew that they really were not necessary. There should be quite a crowd that afternoon.

Chapter Sixteen

The crowd began to gather a full hour early.

There were many more women than had been there the night before, and not a one of them had said a word about their preacher's wife having attended the show. Had things worked out differently, they might have had a great deal to say, most of it unflattering. Under the circumstances, however, it almost seemed that she had done the right thing. And if it was all right for her, it was all right for them.

The Colonel was hard pressed to contain his eagerness.

"What did I tell you?" he said to his wife. She and Louisa were with him in the wagon, waiting for the show to begin. The women never went out until it was time for their parts, the Colonel being a firm believer in not allowing the crowd to see anything ahead of time.

"I expect that the entire town is out there," he went on. "I hope we made up enough of the Miracle Oil and Vitality Pills."

"If we sell all we made, we won't have to give another show for a month," Louisa said. She had helped them in the preparations since they were making an extra large batch. "And if we sell out, you're going to have to get some more bottles and tins. We used nearly all of them."

The Colonel rubbed his hands together. "Last night was not of great financial benefit to us, but I believe we can more than make up for it tonight. Don't you agree, Sophia?"

Sophia had not said much all day. The feeling that they should have left was still strong in her.

"I suppose we can make up for it," she said, but her lack of enthusiasm showed in her face.

"I don't see how you can be worried," the Colonel told her. "Mr. Storey and the others put those rascals to rout last night. They won't be back."

Louisa wanted to say that the rout hadn't been exactly attributable to Mr. Storey, but there was no use. When her father's zealousness was aroused, there was no need in talking to him. He always believed what he wanted to believe, and he almost always painted a prettier picture of things than anyone else would do.

But he was often right, and she supposed that was better than always painting a picture of gloom. In fact, she wished that she could make herself cheer up.

She still could not decide how she felt about Ray Storey. He had not done what she thought was the right thing, but Dr. Stuartson did not seem to see anything wrong in Storey's behavior. She wished that she could make up her mind.

"I think I should go out there and entertain the people for a while before we get to the main part of the show," the Colonel said. "Perhaps a few verses of 'Bury Me Beneath the Willow.'"

He picked up his banjo by the neck and left the wagon.

Sophia sighed.

"Don't worry, Mother," Louisa said. "I'm sure everything will be fine."

"I hope so," Sophia said, but she did not sound hopeful at all.

"That damn cat's under the house," Ben said. He was down on his hands and knees, peering into the dark shadows under the shack. "I can see the bastard in under there, but he won't come out."

"I wish you'd stop worryin' about that cat," Sam said. "He probably knows what you're thinkin' of doin' to him, and he's not about to let you."

"I could shoot him right where he's lyin'," Ben said.

"Just leave him be. We won't be comin' back this way. Maybe he'll starve to death."

That thought cheered Ben momentarily, and he stood up, brushing half heartedly at his pants knees.

"Ain't it about time to go on into town?" he said.

Sam got up from the porch where he had been sitting. "Prob'ly is. It'll be sundown in a couple of hours."

"I hope there ain't gonna be a show," Ben said. "I hope ever' one of them townies is right there at home. It's time to show 'em that they can't mess with us. Nobody oughta mess with the Hawkins brothers."

He kicked a pine cone and sent it skittering under the shack.

"Much less a damn cat," he said. He drew his pistol. "Before we go, I'm gonna shoot that bastard."

"Never mind that scrawny old yellow cat," Sam said. "Take it out on the townies." He started for the lean-to. "Let's saddle up."

Ben watched Sam go and then fired a shot into the dirt under the near edge of the shack. "Take that, you son of a bitch," he said.

No one was much interested in listening to the Colonel's banjo strumming or his singing. They were instead curious about the sheriff and his wounds.

Ray Storey was standing outside the tent, allowing only a few people at a time to go inside, where Dr. Stuartson was attending the sheriff.

Stuartson had drunk his usual quantity that day, or perhaps a little less. He knew better than anyone that no matter what the Colonel's hopes for him, it would take more than one success with a patient to restore him to whatever he had been before he began drinking.

Nevertheless, he had felt an infinitesimal return of self confidence, and he was actually enjoying the attention of the people who came to pay their respects. He was even starting to look forward to presenting the anatomy lecture.

Ray Storey was not looking forward to anything.

He looked in at the sheriff and tried to feel hatred or at least disgust, but he felt nothing. Chet was dead, and there was no way to bring him back. If he killed the sheriff, what difference would that make to Chet?

He wondered if he was just making excuses, for there was no need to try to fool himself.

He was not going to kill the sheriff, even if it would make a difference. He was not a killer. Whatever it took to be one had been left out of his make-up. He had not realized it before because he had been driven by the residue of his rage. But the rage was gone now. The Boozer had been right. There was nothing left but sadness and regret.

Sam and Ben rode into town quietly. There was hardly anyone on the street. The boardwalks on each side were deserted except for a dog sleeping in the sun in front of the saloon and Barclay Sanders, who was sweeping in front of his store.

"I guess there must be another show, all right," Ben said. "Looks like ever'body in town's gone."

"Not ever'body," Sam said. "Let's see what old Sanders has to say for himself."

They rode down the street toward Sanders's store. When they passed the saloon, the dog got up and jumped down into the street. He barked once at the horses, then turned and trotted off.

Sanders, alerted by the dog's bark, looked up. He had not gone to the show because despite having consumed an entire bottle of Miracle Oil, not counting what he had rubbed on his wound, he still had a throbbing headache that just wouldn't go away. He had planned to clean up his store and go home for the day. There was hardly a customer left in town anyway. He would eat a little something and go to bed early. He figured the rest would do him good.

When he saw the two riders coming, the low sun throwing long shadows of them and their horses in the street, he recognized them at once, and he wished mightily that he had gone to the show along with everyone else.

"Well, sir," Ben said when they got to the boardwalk. "Looks like you're all by yourself today."

Sanders looked at them, holding his broom handle clasped in both hands. He was going to stand his ground; he knew there was no use in running.

"You don't look too happy to see us," Ben said. "I bet you thought we were long gone."

That was what Sanders had thought, all right, but he didn't say so. He didn't say anything.

"We figger you owe us some money," Sam said. "You wanta pay up?"

"I don't owe you anything," Sanders said.

"Seems to me like you do," Sam told him. "Seems to me like you haven't paid us in a good long time."

Sanders's shoulders slumped. He should have known that what the Reverend Stump said was too good to be true. There was no way that the town was ever going to be rid of the Hawkinses.

"Just let me go inside," he said. "I'll bring your money. How much is it this time?"

That was too easy for Ben. He'd wanted Sanders to resist a little, at least put up a little bit of a show. He thought he'd try to perk Sanders up.

"All you got," he said, drawing his pistol.

"I can't give you everything," Sanders said. "Hell, you've took near about all of it anyway."

"That's another thing," Sam said. "We took it, but we don't have it now. We want it back."

Sanders straightened. Dammit, they might get what he had in the store, but that was all. He wasn't going to tell them about the money Mrs. Stump had recovered.

"You can just go to hell," he said.

Ben fired twice with his pistol, the twin explosions hammering the air. The first shot went wide, thwacking the wall to Sanders's left, but the second bullet hit Sanders right in the neck.

Sanders dropped the broom, and the handle hit the boardwalk with a thud. Sanders staggered back against the wall, both hands on his neck, but he couldn't stop the blood that was pumping out between his fingers.

He slid slowly down the wall until he was sitting on the boardwalk. He tried to say something, but he couldn't get it out. His mouth was full of blood.

Sam looked at Ben reprovingly. "You didn't need to do that. Now he can't tell us where the money is."

"He oughtn't to tell me to go to hell," Ben said.

"I guess not," Sam said, getting down off his horse. "Hell, the way his head's all bandaged up, it looks like he's been shot once already. I'm going inside and see if he has any money. You wait out here."

Ben waited, looking at Sanders. Blood was soaking the front of Sanders's shirt now, and the storekeeper's eyes were glassy and dead.

"You oughtn't tell a man to go to hell," Ben said, though he didn't figure that Sanders could hear him. He looked down the street to see if the shots had aroused anyone, but no one was coming. They must all have been at the medicine show, he decided. Otherwise, they'd have come running at the shot. Or maybe not. They weren't much good when it came to shooting.

Sam came out of the store. "Just a few dollars," he said. "Better'n nothin', though."

"What're we gonna do about that preacher?" Ben said. "I don't guess he's in town."

"Don't matter if he's gone," Sam said. "The church is still here."

Ben grinned. "Yeah. But maybe it won't be when he gets back."

They turned their horses down the street. From where he sat on the boardwalk, Barclay Sanders seemed to be watching them as they rode away, but his eyes saw nothing.

* * *

There were others in town, of course, but Ben was right about them. They weren't much good when it came to shooting, not even Carl Gary, no matter how much he might have liked people to think so.

He was in his office in the back of the Western Dandy Saloon when he heard the shots. Seeing the medicine show a second time held no interest for him.

He got up, opened the door, and asked the bartender what was going on.

"I don't know," the bartender said. "I just mind my own business."

It was true that he didn't know. He had heard the shots, but he had not moved from behind the bar. If the Hawkins brothers were back in town, he wasn't going to tangle with them.

There was only one patron in the saloon, but he was not interested in the shooting either. He was a serious drinker who had nearly finished a pint of whiskey he had bought earlier. It was possible that he hadn't heard a thing.

Gary walked through the saloon and out the batwing doors. He saw the two men down at the church, but he didn't see Sanders at first.

When he saw him, he had a pretty good idea who the two men were. He crossed the street, first making sure the two riders weren't looking in his direction, and stepped up on the walk in front of Sanders's store.

It was obvious that Sanders was dead. His bloody hands were still at his neck, and the front of his clothing was soaked with red.

Gary felt that he should do something, get Sanders inside maybe, but he didn't want to get the blood all over him. He would have to go for Tal Thurman, if Tal wasn't at the medicine show and assuming that Sam and Ben didn't come after him before he could locate the undertaker.

He wondered what those two were doing down by the church.

Then he heard shooting again.

*   *   *

Sam first threw a loop of his lasso around part of the picket fence, then dragged it into the street.

That wasn't very satisfactory, however, so he and Ben drew their pistols and started shooting out the windows of the church. It was a little disappointing that there were so few colored ones, but they saved those for last. Sam, being the better shot, got most of them, but Ben enjoyed watching the glass splinter and fall.

Even breaking the windows did not pacify the Hawkinses. Sam could not forget how that preacher had made him run.

As he thumbed fresh cartridges into his pistol, he wondered what else he could do. It didn't take him long to think of something. He got down from his horse and opened the door of the church.

"Go right on in, Ben," he said. "A little religion will do you good."

Ben went in, all right, but he did not get off his horse. The church door was wide and high, and he rode right through.

As his horse clopped down the narrow center aisle, Ben fired his pistol into the lectern that stood on the dais behind the altar. He fired at the pews. He fired at the walls.

Sam walked in behind him, his pistol blasting at the ceiling, at the little shards of glass that still hung in the windows.

The thunder of the shots echoed in the church, and smoke filled the sanctuary before it began to eddy out the empty windows.

By the time the Hawkins brothers emerged from the church, Carl Gary was gone from town. He was on his way to the medicine show.

Barclay Sanders still sat in front of his store, his blank eyes staring at nothing.

Chapter Seventeen

Colonel A. J. Mahaffey thought the crowd was the largest he had ever seen at one of his shows. They were going to sell a lot of Miracle Oil

Storey had been reluctant to perform the shooting exhibition, but the Colonel had insisted, and things had gone well. Storey had been as good as he had ever been, and the only thing that worried the Colonel was that after the shooting Storey went behind the wagon and reloaded his pistols.

Storey didn't know why he did it, either. He didn't think there would be any occasion to use them, and he didn't think he would use them if the occasion arose. But he reloaded nevertheless.

Banju Ta-Ta did her dance again, with as much fervor as ever, and possibly more.

The Squaw Ro-Shanna repeated her story about the unusual rabbits, this time adding a few details that had not been included the previous day but that the Colonel had thought might improve the performance.

Sophia had thought that people might notice, but no one seemed to.

One reason that things went so well might have been Sheriff Wilson, who came out of the tent and watched the show from a bench that Storey and Stuartson had moved outside for him. He wasn't strong enough to walk easily and had to be assisted by Storey and Stuartson, but his presence seemed to reinforce the wonderful healing qualities of the Miracle Oil.

There was no doubt that the Colonel would have sold more than a hundred bottles, in spite of the fact that everyone had bought a bottle the day before, except for one thing.

That one thing was Carl Gary, who came riding up just as the Colonel was about to begin his pitch.

Gary's horse was lathered, and the saloon owner had lost his hat on the road. His hair was sticking out wildly, and no one in the crowd could ever remember having seen him so discomposed.

He reined in just at the edge of the crowd and started yelling about the Hawkins brothers.

"They're tearing up the town!" he said. "They've killed Barclay Sanders, and they're wrecking the church!"

"The church?" Lawton Stump said. He felt a horrible weight settle on his shoulders. It was his punishment for taking up the gun.

"They rode inside on their horses, shooting," Gary said, and Stump felt the weight settle harder.

Naomi put her arms around him. "We can fix it again," she said. "We can work together."

Stump did not seem comforted, but the other citizens were not as worried about the church as they were about what the Hawkins brothers might do next. They voiced their concern, and Carl Gary said, "There's nobody in town left for them to shoot, not that they care about shooting. I think they might come here."

Gary was right; that was exactly what Sam and Ben were planning to do.

They took some time at first, however, to look in on the saloon for a minute. The bartender had been instructed by Gary before he left to give them whatever they wanted. Gary had assured the man that there would be no trouble as long as Sam and Ben were not crossed, though he had not mentioned the condition of the late Barclay Sanders.

When Sam and Ben entered, guns drawn, the dedicated drinker at the table picked up what was left of his pint and faded silently as a shadow out the back door of the saloon. The Hawkins brothers never even saw him.

"What can I do for you fellas?" the bartender said in a voice that he had to work to keep steady.

"We'll take all your money," Sam said, and the bartender immediately handed over everything that was in his cash drawer. He was going to follow Gary's instructions completely. Gary had been careful to leave an amount that he hoped would appease the Hawkinses.

"Fifty-six dollars," Sam said, counting it. "Not bad for one place." Satisfied, he shoved the money in the pocket of his Levi's. "Now we want some of your whiskey."

"Not the bar stuff, either," Ben said, holding his pistol so that it was pointed at the bartender's head. "The stuff you keep for your boss to drink is what we want."

The fact was that Carl Gary did not drink. He did not see the point in it. If others wanted to do so, that was fine, but he chose not to partake himself.

The bartender didn't try to explain any of that to Ben. He simply reached under the bar, brought out a fancy cut-glass bottle and handed it to him.

"This better be your best stuff," Ben said, taking it with his left hand and continuing to aim his pistol with his right. He looked at the bottle with approval, holding it up so that Sam could admire it as well.

"It's the best we got," the bartender said. He didn't really think Ben could tell the difference if it wasn't, but once again he hadn't taken any chances.

Ben uncorked the bottle and tilted it to his mouth.

He coughed, then said, "Damn that's smooth. You want a little taste, Sam?"

Sam did. He had a swallow, and then Ben had another for himself.

Then Ben plunked the bottle down hard on the bar. "I guess you were tellin' the truth. That's about the best whiskey I ever drank."

"Yeah," the bartender said. "It's supposed to be good."

"Just for that, I'm not gonna kill you," Ben said, and opened fire with his pistol.

Behind the bar there was a long mirror, and on each side of it were glass shelves holding various bottles of amber fluid. Ben shot five of the bottles in rapid succession, sending glass and whiskey flying. He put his sixth bullet into the center of the mirror, or close to it, sending a spider web of cracks across its face.

"We look pretty damn silly, don't we, Sam?" he said, eyeing their reflections in the cracked glass. A jagged line ran across their bearded faces, making it appear that the top halves sat slightly to the sides of the bottoms.

"Yeah," Sam said. He looked at the bartender, who had not turned to see the mirror. He was still shaken by the shots. "Where is ever'body today?"

"Out at the medicine show," the bartender said, wishing that he was there too.

"Guess we oughta head on out that way, then," Sam said. The bartender had confirmed what he suspected.

"Damn right," Ben said, grabbing the neck of the whiskey bottle and lifting it from the bar. "Let's pay ever'body a little visit."

As they left the saloon, the bartender changed his mind. He didn't wish he was at the medicine show after all.

The crowd was in a dither. No one seemed to know what to do or where to go. They looked first to Carl Gary for leadership, but he was not equipped to provide it.

It was one thing to confront the sheriff and demand that he take a posse to roust the Hawkins brothers, but it was another thing to know that the Hawkinses were coming your way with blood on their minds. Gary wanted no part of it, and he said so.

"You people can't expect me to stand up to those two. It's not my responsibility. Anyway, it's not me they're after, judging from what they were doing to that church."

Then everyone looked to Coy Wilson. The seven people who knew the truth about Wilson's relationship with the brothers knew that this would be a real test for the sheriff, and they knew that if he did not pass it they would have to tell what they knew. On the other hand, if he demonstrated that he had indeed changed for the better, they would give him the opportunity to redeem himself. The money he had extorted from the townspeople could be discussed later.

Wilson struggled to get off the bench where he had been sitting. "I stood up to 'em once," he said. His voice was weak but firm. "And I'll do it again. Course I'd be mighty glad if some of you was to stand up with me, considerin' the way things turned out the last time."

He didn't really expect anyone to agree to help him. He hadn't been a good sheriff, had in fact been something of a bully, and he knew that no one liked him very much. Why should they? He had betrayed them in ways that they didn't even know about. Nevertheless, he knew that he could no longer be a part of what Sam and Ben stood for.

Maybe it had all started back in Kansas when he ran down that kid. He'd never been able to get that out of his mind. Or maybe it had started later on, when he saw that a decent life was actually a possibility for him. Maybe he was just getting old. For whatever reason, he had to stand up to Sam and Ben now, no matter what.

"I'll stand with you," Ray Storey said, and no one was more surprised than he was that he'd said it. In the first place, he didn't know what good he'd be. And in the second place, this was the man that had been responsible for Chet's death. None of that seemed to matter, however, as Storey walked over to stand by Wilson.

That decided matters for everyone from town. There were two men with guns against two other men with guns. There was no need for them to stay around.

"We've got the women to think of," a man said. "We better get them in the wagons and get back to town."

"We've got property back there to look after," Carl Gary said, thinking of his saloon and wondering if it was still in operating condition. He thought briefly about his bartender and hoped that the Hawkins brothers hadn't killed him. It was hard to find good bartenders.

"What if we meet the Hawkinses on the road?" a woman said.

"We can go around by the old Wilton trail," Gary said. "I came out that way so they wouldn't come up behind me."

No one bothered to point out that by taking that route he might have been too late to warn them, considering that the Wilton trail was a mile or more longer than the usual route to the waterhole. Everyone was too busy climbing into wagons and mounting horses to think about that.

Before too long there was nothing except a lingering dust cloud in the air to remind anyone of their presence.

"Well," the Colonel said as the last of them departed, "it appears that my expectations of a successful show are not to be realized. You were right, Sophia. We should have left yesterday."

"There's still time," she said. "We can hitch the team and leave before they get here."

"We could try to run," he said. "But we would have to leave the tent behind. Besides, they would catch us easily."

"You folks better at least get in your show wagon," Wilson said.

"I think we ought to do something to help," Louisa said. "I don't want to hide from those men. I'm not afraid."

"You better be," Wilson said. "They wouldn't want to kill you if they could help it, but you wouldn't like what they'd want to do instead."

"You and your mother get inside the wagon," the Colonel said to his daughter. "The doctor and I will be along directly."

"You come now," Sophia said.

"I'll be along. Don't worry about me."

Sophia gave her husband a short look. "All right. Come with me, Louisa."

Louisa looked as if she would like to say more, but she followed her mother.

"Now," the Colonel said to Wilson. "What is it that you propose to do, exactly?"

"Face up to 'em," Wilson said, unable to think of anything else. "That's all we can do."

"That didn't seem to avail you much last evening," the Colonel told him. "And now you're not exactly in fighting condition."

"You got a better idea?" Wilson said.

The Colonel shook his head. "Unfortunately not."

Wilson forced a smile. "Well, then."

The Boozer looked at Ray Storey. "What about you?" he said. "How do you feel about this?"

"I'd feel better if we had a few more people backing us up," Storey said. "I didn't think everyone would go off like that."

"They've never wanted to stand up to Sam and Ben before," Wilson said. "They ain't gonna start now."

"Perhaps they weren't encouraged to stand up to them," the Colonel suggested.

Wilson gave him a shrewd glance. "How much do you know about that?"

"Quite a bit. The reverend Stump's wife overheard you talking to those reprobates last night."

Wilson sighed. "I was afraid of that. I guess it don't do much good to say that I'm sorry about what I did. It's too late for that."

"It may not be," The Boozer said. "People can sometimes be very forgiving. You might find that to be the case here."

"It may not matter, not when Sam and Ben get through with me," Wilson said. "I was just tryin' to get rid of them and get on with my life when I sent 'em out here last night."

"You sent them?" the Colonel said.

"I hoped they'd take your money and just leave, go on back to Kansas. I shoulda known that it wouldn't work like that."

"No, it didn't," the Colonel said. "It might have, though, and I suppose the money I lost would have been a small price to pay."

"Maybe," Wilson said. "I'd still feel better if some of those folks had stuck around to help me."

"Maybe they did," Storey said. "Here comes a wagon."

It wasn't a wagon that Storey had heard. It was Stump's buggy. The preacher drove into the clearing and stopped.

"I couldn't go back to town," he said. "Not and leave you here to face those men alone. It would not have been right."

Naomi sat beside him, holding his arm. She was frightened, but she was thrilled that her husband had proved to be so brave.

"Are you armed?" the Colonel said.

"No," Stump said. "But I don't require a six-gun to stand up to skunks."

"Maybe not, but I'd sure advise one," Wilson said. "The skunks'll have 'em."

Stump got out of the buggy and helped his wife down.

"She can go into the show wagon with my wife and daughter," the Colonel said. He walked over to her and guided her inside.

"I thought they might have gotten here by now," Stump said, joining Wilson and Storey.

"So did I," Wilson said. "It ain't like them to be late to a fight."

"Could they have gotten lost on the way?" the Colonel said, having stowed Naomi safely in the wagon.

"Not them two," Wilson said. "It's a plain trail, and they know the way, day or night."

The afternoon sun was nearly below the horizon. The trees cast deep shadows over the medicine show wagon and those standing near it. The full moon, white and huge, was already in the sky. There were no clouds.

"Looks like we'll be able to see them when they come," Wilson said.

Storey nodded. He didn't know whether that was good or bad. He just wished that Stump had a pistol. Or that he was sure that he would use his own.

Chapter Eighteen

The Boozer, had he known what Sam and Ben were doing, could have explained their delay in arriving. They had partaken heavily of the whiskey in the cut glass bottle, passing it back and forth as they rode until nearly all of it was gone. They had eaten little that day, and the whiskey took effect quickly, especially with Ben, who was less able to deal with alcohol than Sam was.

Ben's eyes were bleary and red, and there was a trickle of whiskey running through his beard from the left corner of his mouth. He had drunk so much that he was actually beginning to regret having shot Coy Wilson.

"He was all right when he wasn't being so damn uppity," Ben said. "I wish you hadn't killed him, Sam."

Sam was not as affected as Ben, but he was feeling a bit dizzy. The motion of the horse was no comfort to his spinning head, and he did not feel like taking the blame for Wilson's imagined death.

"I didn't kill him, you sorry bastard," Sam said. "You did. I just winged him. You're the one that killed him."

Ben, who happened to be the one holding the bottle at the time, heaved it at his brother's head.

Sam ducked back, but it struck him a glancing blow on the forehead, cutting a long gash just under his hat brim and nearly knocking him off his horse.

As soon as he regained his balance, Sam jerked his reins and rode his horse into Ben's as hard as he could, at the same time reaching for Ben with the intention of dragging him from the saddle.

Ben fought back with bobcat ferocity, ducking under Sam's thrashing arms and butting Sam in the sternum with the top of his head.

Ben's hat softened the blow a little, but not enough for Sam, who leaned back, gagging for breath.

Ben did not waste time or sentiment in following up his advantage. He balled up his thick fingers and smashed Sam on the side of the head.

Sam tumbled off his horse and fell hard. Ben jumped down after him, prepared to kick him in the stomach or kidneys, but Sam was on his knees spewing most of the whiskey he had drunk into the dirt.

"Phew," Ben said, turning away in disgust. He started looking for the bottle, wondering if there might be a swallow or two left in it. He was no longer interested in Sam.

He found the bottle lying on its side near the trail. There was a thin puddle of whiskey inside.

Ben was reaching for the bottle when someone dropped a tree on him, or at least that was what it felt like. Actually, it was only Sam, who was through retching and mad as hell.

He bore Ben down, sat astraddle of him, tore his hat off, and began pummeling the back of his head. With each blow, Ben's face bounced off the hard dirt of the trail. A stream of blood began to flow from his nose, which was taking most of the punishment.

"You son of a bitch," Sam said. "I didn't kill Coy. You did it. Say you did it."

The blows on his head, or possibly the contact of his nose with the ground, had a sobering and cleansing effect on Ben's mind. He came up with an idea that he was sure would impress his brother.

"Maybe we didn't either one of us kill him," he said, or tried to say. It was hard to understand him because his mouth had quite a bit or dirt in it.

Sam caught part of it and stopped hitting him.

"Huh?" he said. He did not get off Ben, however.

Ben raised his head and spit out dirt and some of the bile that had risen in his throat. He would have wiped his nose, but Sam had his arms pinned to his sides.

"I said, maybe we didn't either one of us kill him."

Sam hit him in the back of the head, but not very hard this time. "You can't get out of it that way."

"It's the truth," Ben said. "If we did, why is ever'body at the medicine show? Why ain't there a funeral."

That made Sam think. But not for long. "They had it before we got there," he said.

Ben craned his neck and tried to look around at Sam. "Didn't nobody say anything about it. Not Sanders or that bartender either one. We musta just winged him, and he played possum on us."

Sam thought about that. His head was no longer spinning from the whiskey. He started to think that Ben might even be right.

"If he ain't dead," he said, "where the hell is he?"

Ben had already thought of an answer for that one.

"I bet he's at the medicine show with the rest of them," he said.

Sam stood, freeing Ben's arms and stepping away from him.

Ben rolled over on his back and sat up, brushing at his bleeding nose with the sleeve of his shirt. He left a smear of blood and dirt under his nose. His beard was full of dirt, but he didn't bother with that, though he did pick out a small stick that was bothering him. He looked around for his hat, which was lying nearby. He grabbed it and mashed it down on his head.

"You know something, Ben?" Sam said.

"No," Ben said. "What?"

"You may be a son of a bitch, but sometimes you're smarter than you look."

"That's good," Ben said, standing up. "I'm sorry I threw that whiskey bottle at you, Sam."

Sam touched his forehead, where an egg-sized lump had formed. "Me too," he said.

"What're we gonna do about Coy?" Ben said.

"We're gonna see if he's at that medicine show," Sam said.

"What if he is?"

"This time, we're gonna kill him for sure."

"I'll do it if you don't want to," Ben said. He wanted to make up for throwing the bottle.

"Don't worry about that," Sam said. "I want to kill him, all right. And all the rest of those sorry bastards with him."

Ben grinned. It sounded like a good plan to him.

Storey wondered why the Colonel and The Boozer were still outside the wagon.

"Since you don't have pistols, you'd be a lot safer inside," he said.

"The preacher doesn't have a gun," the Colonel said. "And he does not appear to be going inside."

Storey had never known the Colonel to wear a gun, didn't even think the man owned one except for a rifle that he kept in the wagon. For someone who had expressed no interest in the military life that went with his assumed title, he was demonstrating a kind of courage that Storey equated with foolhardiness.

"They did not shoot me last evening," the Colonel pointed out. "Why should they do it this time?" He believed that in facing up to Sam and Ben he had cowed them in some way, and he believed he could do it again.

"You can't tell what they might do," Wilson said. "They've killed men before, plenty of 'em. They tried to kill me."

"This is my show, and my wagon," the Colonel said. "I'm not going to hide from them." Clearly he meant it. He wasn't going inside.

"I guess I won't hide either," The Boozer said. He thought, but did not add, that he really didn't have much to lose. The thought of getting killed didn't bother him in the least. There were times when it actually appealed to him, and this was one of those times.

"You're both crazy," Wilson said. "But I appreciate you standing with me."

Actually, Wilson was not standing now. He was sitting back down on the bench. He didn't feel like being on his feet any more than he had to.

Storey sat down beside him. "Do you remember riding down a kid back in a Kansas street after a bank robbery a year or so back?" he said, speaking quietly so the others would not overhear.

Wilson scrubbed his face with his hands. "Yeah, I remember. Did that preacher's wife tell you that, too?"

"That kid was my brother," Storey said. "His name was Chet."

"My God," Wilson said.

"I've been looking for you a long time," Storey told him. "I thought it was Sam Hawkins I was looking for, but it was you all along."

"I'm sorry," Wilson said. "God, I never meant to ride him down. There was shootin' and yellin' all around, and we were ridin' hard to get out of that damn place, and then he was just right there in front of me. I tried to swerve off when I saw him, but it was too late."

"He thought the shots were fireworks," Storey said. "He was running to see the fireworks."

Wilson didn't say anything for a minute. Then he said, "Why're you here with me now? You've got the only other gun. Why don't you just leave me here? You don't even have to kill me yourself. Sam and Ben will take care of me for you."

"I wanted to kill you once," Storey said. "But not anymore. What happened wasn't even your fault. I know that now."

"I don't know if I could ever feel that way," Wilson said. "Not if somebody killed my brother."

"I didn't know I could feel that way, either. But I do."

"And you're gonna help me?"

169

"As much as I can," Storey said, wondering just how much that was going to be.

"Where the hell is ever'body," Ben said. He and Sam had ridden off the trail and into the trees to look the situation over. "You don't reckon they're all hidin' and waitin' for us do you?"

Sam knew that wasn't the case. Those townies were gutless as a gopher.

"They musta heard we were on the way and left," he said. "Prob'ly went back to town the long way around so they wouldn't run into us."

Despite his conviction that there was no one there except those they could see near the wagon, Sam's eyes were scanning the trees and the shadows, checking to see if anyone was concealed in them. He had no intention of being surprised.

But he could see no one there.

"Just the five of 'em," he said. "That's all."

"Looks like three of 'em don't even have guns," Ben said. "And old Coy don't look too pert. I reckon he's got a bullet or two in him."

"That buckskin fella ain't fired a shot at us yet, either," Sam said. "I don't think we got much to worry about from him. Looks like easy pickin's to me."

"Where do you reckon the women are?" Ben said. "That Injun girl was mighty spirited. I don't know as I trust her not to have a gun or a knife."

"Prob'ly inside the wagon," Sam said.

"You think we'll have time for the women?" Ben said. "I don't think any of those townies'll come after us, and it'll take a long time to get any other law on our tails."

"We'll have a look in the wagon," Sam said. "Could be that our money's in there if the preacher's wife is." He smiled. "I guess it wouldn't be a bad idea to search her pretty close. The others, too."

"Yeah," Ben said. "When we gonna do it?"

"Now," Sam said.

Chapter Nineteen

They came without warning, riding hard out of the trees, their pistols spitting flame and lead.

The Boozer went down first, spinning around and slamming against one of the wagon wheels. The Colonel leapt to him and knelt beside him, cradling his head in his arms.

Wilson was next, dropped from the bench where he sat, his pistol falling from his suddenly limp fingers.

The Reverend Stump fell to his knees. He was not hit, however. He was retrieving Wilson's pistol.

Storey, to his immense shock, found that his own gun was in his hand and that he was firing it as rapidly as he could, sending shot after shot in the direction of the charging horses. He hadn't even been conscious of drawing the weapon, and he was hardly aware of having fired it.

Then Sam and Ben were by them, roaring toward the trees on the other side of the clearing.

Storey spit to get the dust out of his mouth and cleared the cylinder of his Colt, dropping the casings on the ground and thumbing in fresh cartridges.

Stump sent a couple of wild shots after the Hawkinses from his position beside Wilson, emptying the pistol; then he started popping shells from Wilson's cartridge belt to reload.

Ben and Sam were reloading as well.

"I thought you said that buckskin bastard wouldn't shoot," Ben said. "He like to've shot me out of the damn saddle."

"He didn't, though," Sam said.

"I think we got old Coy that time," Ben said. "I guess it was me that done it."

Sam didn't know whether Ben was taking the credit or the blame, but he didn't want to argue about it.

"Sure," he said. "Now let's get the rest of them."

They turned their horses back and attacked the clearing again just as Louisa stepped out of the wagon with the rifle, a Winchester repeater.

"Thank you, my dear," the Colonel said, letting The Boozer's head down gently and rising to take the rifle from her. "I suppose I'm going to have to use this."

He was no better shot than Stump, but a rifle was something for Sam and Ben to reckon with. He blasted a couple of rounds into the dirt in front of the running horses, then raised his sights and sent one over the Hawkins brothers' heads.

Stump fired a shot that somehow clipped Ben's reins. Ben's horse swerved aside just in time to save Ben from being killed by a shot from Storey, but the horse was running wild now, carrying Ben away into the trees. The Colonel loosed a round after him but hit nothing more than the branch of a pine tree, snipping it off the trunk. It brushed by Ben when it fell.

Storey raised his pistol almost without thinking and fired a shot at Sam that hit him squarely in the center of the chest, lifting him six inches in the air and throwing him backward from the saddle.

There was a look of terrible surprise in Sam's eyes as he hit the ground, a look that turned to a grimace of pain as he tried to stand. His knees were watery, and he could not seem able to lift his pistol. He kept trying, however, and Storey shot him again, sending him stumbling backward.

He fell sprawling in the dirt and this time he didn't try to get up.

Storey's ears were ringing from the firing as he walked over and looked down at Sam. There were two dark, spreading stains on the front of his filthy shirt. Sam's eyes stared blankly up at the rising moon.

Storey holstered his Colt and reached down to feel for a pulse in the side of Sam's neck. There was none, and Storey imagined that Sam's body was already cooling.

Here's the man I wanted to kill for so long, Storey thought, *and now I've killed him.*

The trouble was that as things had turned out Sam was the wrong man, and Storey hadn't wanted to kill him anymore.

When he'd wanted to do it, he hadn't been able; when he'd found out that Sam hadn't been the right one after all, he'd shot him. Somehow it seemed that when he'd stopped thinking about it, his body had just taken over and done it.

I guess I wasn't a coward after all, Storey thought.

Storey was neither glad nor sad about that. Having just killed a man didn't make a lot of difference to him, either. Sam had been trying to kill Storey, and now Sam was dead. That seemed a fair exchange to Storey, and if Sam felt any different, well, he wasn't going to be telling anyone.

Storey turned back to see about Wilson and The Boozer. Sophia and Louisa had joined the Colonel at The Boozer's side, while Naomi and Stump were looking after Wilson, not that anyone could be of much help to either man.

The Boozer had been hit in the chest, much like Sam Hawkins. He was still alive, but only barely.

He looked up at Storey. "Do you remember what I said about knowing when the time had come?" he said. His voice was weak and raspy.

"I remember," Storey said.

"Good," The Boozer said. "Now you know what I was talking about."

Louisa looked at Storey. She understood even if he didn't.

"I guess I do," Storey said, though he really wasn't sure.

The Boozer didn't have any more to say. His head slumped back and his breathing stopped.

Wilson was as good as dead, too, shot in the stomach this time. He lingered for a bit longer than The Boozer, however, and his pain was worse. He didn't seem to mind that part. He had something else on his mind.

"I really am sorry about your brother," he told Storey.

"It's all right," Storey said. He was sure about that. "It was just an accident."

"I shouldn't have been there for it to happen," Wilson said.

"Maybe Chet shouldn't have been there. All I know is that I don't blame you for it any longer," Storey said.

"That's good to know," Wilson said. "About that money Sam and Ben and I took, Preacher—"

"What about it?" Stump said.

"I still have most of it. It's in the safe at the jail. I'd be obliged if you could see that folks get it back."

"I'll do my best," Stump said.

"Thanks," Wilson said. "I 'preciate it."

He closed his eyes and didn't say any more. In a few minutes he was dead.

The Reverend Stump closed Wilson's eyes and put his pistol back in its holster. For a wonder he didn't feel guilty about having taken it up, and he knew that the destruction in his church, no matter what its extent, was not a result of his having done so the first time. A man can turn the other cheek when he's slapped, but when he's shot at he sometimes has to shoot back.

"I believe we should go back to town and check on things," he told Naomi. "We have a lot of work to do."

"I for one am not entirely convinced that your town is worth it," the Colonel said. He had liked The Boozer quite a bit more than he had ever put into words.

"It's worth it," Stump said. "The people there are no better or no worse than those anywhere. They are simply dedicated to their own survival, as are most of us."

"Not all, though," Sophia said. "You stayed to help, Mr. Stump."

"I didn't stay. I came back," he reminded her. "My first impulse was to leave like the rest."

"But you did return," the Colonel said. "We thank you for that."

"You are most welcome," Stump said. "Believe me, I have received as much from you as you have gotten from me."

"Then that is the way things are supposed to work," the Colonel said. "We would appreciate it if you would send the undertaker for our friend Dr. Stuartson and the sheriff. I will pay for the burial of Dr. Stuartson."

"I would be honored to conduct his service," Stump said.

The Colonel felt that was an excellent idea.

"The town will take care of the sheriff," Stump said. "There's no need for them to know the things Naomi learned."

"Of course not," his wife said. "He proved his worth at the last. We can get that money from the jail and put it with the rest that I found last night."

"As for the other man lying over there—" the Colonel said.

"As for him, Tal Thurman can shovel him under the best way he can," Stump said. "The man is not deserving of a Christian burial. And as for Ben—"

"I hope we've seen the last of him," Naomi said. "Surely he won't return after this."

"Remember what Wilson said," Storey told them. "You can't tell what Ben might do."

Stump nodded agreement. "That is a sad fact," he said.

Ben was watching them from the trees, having gotten control of his horse and returned after tying the reins together.

He could see them, every one, outlined sharply by the bright light of the hovering moon.

He could see Sam's body more clearly than anything as it lay apart from the others, totally disregarded by everyone.

Large round tears rolled from his eyes and into his matted beard. "Goddammit, Sam," he said. "They killed you, Sam, goddammit."

They were going to be sorry for that, he promised himself. He was going to make them sorry.

He watched as they picked up the bodies of The Boozer and Coy Wilson and laid them out head to head on the bench where Wilson had been sitting.

They left Sam lying in the dirt.

He watched as Stump fetched his buggy and helped Naomi up. Then he knew what he was going to do.

"I'll ride back to town with you," Storey said. "Just in case Ben Hawkins is out there somewhere." He didn't know how much protection he would offer. Having done something once did not mean he could do it again. But he figured that having a man with a gun riding along would be better than having no gun at all.

"We'd be grateful for your company," Stump said. "But what about your friends here?"

"They can get inside the wagon. That'll give them plenty of protection. And they have the rifle."

"I'm not enough of a marksman to be much of a threat to anyone," the Colonel said. "But the wagon is solid. No one will be able to get inside."

Storey went to saddle his horse. Louisa followed him.

"I want you to know that I understand what happened tonight," she said.

"That's good," Storey told her. "I don't."

"Never mind," she said. "You will." She put a hand on his arm to stop him. When he looked at her, she stood on tiptoe and kissed his cheek. Then she turned and walked back to the wagon.

Storey watched her go. He understood *that*, all right, and he knew that his relationship with Louisa had changed considerably in the last day or so. To his surprise, he found that he was happy about it.

He had often wondered what he would do if he ever found Sam Hawkins and killed him. Now he knew. At least for a little while, he would continue to be the Colonel's Kit Carson. Maybe for a long time.

He saddled his horse, joined the Stumps, and they headed back into town.

Ben was waiting for them.

He had expected only the preacher and his wife, but he didn't mind at all seeing Storey. That just made things that much better. He could kill him and then take care of the other two.

Having seen Storey shoot and kill Sam, Ben didn't plan to give Storey a chance to do the same for him. He drew his pistol and shot from the concealment of the trees.

He was gratified to see Storey fall sideways from his horse and hit the ground with a thud.

The preacher's wife screamed, and the Reverend Stump grabbed his whip and touched up his horse, but it didn't do any good. Ben raced past where Storey had fallen and caught Stump and Naomi before they'd gone fifty yards, reaching down and grabbing the reins and bringing the buggy to a halt.

"Well, now, preacher," he said, pointing his pistol at Stump's head. "It's not neighborly to run off from your friends like that."

"You are no friend of ours," Stump said, moving in the seat to position himself protectively in front of Naomi.

"Yeah, I guess you're sure enough right about that," Ben said. He flipped his pistol in the air, grasping it with his hand around the cylinder and slamming the butt into the side of Stump's head.

The butt met bone with a cracking sound, and as Stump crumpled forward Ben grabbed his arm and dragged him off the buggy seat, letting him fall to the ground on his face.

Naomi gasped as her husband fell, but she did not panic. She reached for the buggy whip instead.

Ben flipped the pistol again and pointed it at her.

"No use in you tryin' anything," he said. "Just lay that whip down and get outta the buggy."

Naomi fixed him with a hard stare. "No," she said.

Ben cocked his pistol. "I got plans for you, but I don't much mind killin' you first," he said. "That ain't gonna stop me from doin' anything else I wanta do. I just hope your husband wakes up by then so he can watch me."

He grinned at Naomi and winked. "And when I'm finished with you, I'm gonna go back and do that little Injun girl."

"No, you're not." It was Ray Storey. He was walking toward the buggy, his right arm hanging useless at his side. His face was gray in the moonlight, and the sleeve of his buckskin outfit was black with blood. He was holding his revolver in his left hand.

Ben threw his head back and laughed. "You're a sorry sight," he said. "You think you can stop me?"

Storey didn't know. He didn't shoot especially well with his right hand, and he didn't really want to risk a shot with his left. He was just as likely to hit the preacher's wife as to hit Ben.

So he didn't say anything. He just kept walking.

"You take a lot of killin'," Ben said. "But I'm willin' to keep tryin'."

He fired at Storey again, and by pure luck his bullet struck Storey's pistol.

The pistol spun away, and Storey did not look for it. He knew that it would be useless. His arm and hand were numbed from the shock of having the pistol twisted from him by the bullet, but he kept on walking forward.

Naomi, taking advantage of the distraction, picked up the reins and snapped the whip. the buggy jumped forward.

"Goddammit!" Ben said, seeing his plans going wrong and feeling terribly confused.

He tried to think of what he should do. He wished Sam were there to tell him. He didn't know whether to go after Naomi, shoot Stump where he was lying, or shoot Storey. If only those bastards hadn't killed Sam!

He hesitated just long enough for Storey, breaking into a shambling run, to reach him.

Storey had almost no feeling in the fingers of his right hand, but he had enough to grab a handful of Ben's Levi's and pull.

Ben fired a shot uselessly into the air as Storey pulled him from the saddle.

Ben hit the ground on his back, and Storey fell on him, trying to get a grip on Ben's hairy neck.

He could not, and Ben clubbed at his head with the pistol barrel. For one of the first times he could remember, Storey was thankful for the beaver hat the Colonel wanted him to wear. It had cushioned most of the blow.

Seeing that he wasn't getting anywhere, Ben pulled the trigger. Storey felt the bullet burn by his ear and butted Ben in the chin.

Ben's beard absorbed most of the force of the blow, but his teeth clicked together as his head snapped back, hitting the ground.

He didn't stop his struggles. He writhed beneath Storey like a frenzied snake. Storey could smell sour sweat and rancid breath.

Ben, finally remembering that Storey was wounded, began beating at Storey's shoulder with his fist.

Lightning bolts of pain flashed down Storey's right arm and into his finger tips. More pain radiated out from the shoulder into Storey's chest and back.

Storey yelled but did not roll off Ben. He kept himself on top by holding on with his good arm, which really wasn't all that good.

Ben continued to pound the wound, at the same time trying to work the barrel of his pistol up under Storey's chin. He was going to blow off the top of Storey's head.

Storey knew what was happening, but he was determined not to let Ben get up. If he did, Ben would kill him for sure, and the others too.

He tried to keep his head moving, to butt Ben's chin again. He thought that if he could hold Ben down long enough, he might be able to wear him out. It didn't seem likely, however. He didn't know how much more punishment his arm could take.

Ben was not wearing out. He was like a trapped animal, his rage feeding his strength. He would never give up.

He got his pistol in position and pulled the trigger.

Chapter Twenty

The Reverend Stump was seeing double, or maybe triple. He wasn't sure. There were more moons in the sky than there should be, though; he could tell that much. His head felt as if a horse had stepped on it.

He heard the sounds of a struggle nearby and the memory of what had happened returned in a rush.

Naomi!

He sat up suddenly, looking around quickly. His head nearly came apart, and he clutched it with his hands to hold it together.

There was no sign of either the buggy or Naomi, but he could see the two men wrestling in the dirt not so far away. Or maybe there were four of them. It wasn't easy to be sure.

One thing he could see, however, was that one of the men—or two of them—was Mr. Storey. The buckskin outfit was hard to forget.

The other man, then, had to be Ben Hawkins.

Stump crawled over to them and seized Ben's arm, wrenching it aside as Ben pulled the trigger to blow off Storey's head.

This bullet came close to doing its job, tearing its way through

Storey's long hair and nipping off the lobe of his left ear. Blood dripped down onto Ben's chest as he thrashed under Storey and tried to tear his arm out of Stump's grip.

Stump proved to be more tenacious than Ben might have expected. He refused to release his hold.

Storey was glad for the preacher's help, but he didn't know whether even the two of them were going to be able to subdue the furious Ben.

Then Storey thought of something else. The skinning knife. He had not unsheathed it for weeks, probably longer, but it was still there. If he could get it in his hand and hold onto it, they might have a chance.

His fingers touched the handle, and he was surprised that he could feel it so well. The numbness was beginning to wear off.

He pulled out the knife and brought it up, fighting against Ben's twisting body, pushing it through Ben's beard and into the bottom of his chin.

Ben stopped struggling almost immediately. The sharp point of the knife in a particularly soft and vulnerable spot altered his strategy. He knew that if he continued to flail around, he might cause his own death.

"Drop the pistol," Storey said.

"Sure," Ben said, letting the pistol go. "It's dropped."

"All right, Preacher," Storey said. "Let's get him up now. But don't let go of that arm."

They stood Ben up, Storey keeping the point of the knife pressed into the tender skin. Stump slipped once, causing the point to sink in deeper. Storey didn't try to ease it out.

"You killed a good friend of mine tonight," Storey said. "And the sheriff was supposed to be a friend of yours. I guess we might as well kill you."

He punched the point of the knife in just a little deeper.

Ben rose up on his toes. "You killed Sam," he said. His voice was quavery.

"Sam was armed," Storey said. "The Boo—Dr. Stuartson

wasn't. He never hurt anybody." He pushed the knife in a little farther still. It was hard to keep himself from ramming it right on through, through the mouth and into the brain.

Killing Sam had been hard; killing Ben was going to be easy.

"Vengeance belongs to the Lord," Stump said, recovering enough to talk now. "There's no need to murder this man."

"I thought you were shooting a pistol at him not long ago," Storey said, relaxing slightly.

"That was different." Stump echoed his own earlier thoughts. "There is a season for fighting back and even a time for killing. But there is a time for other things, as well."

Storey was reminded of what Stuartson had told him, and all at once it began to make more sense. There was indeed a time to fight back, and Storey had finally learned when that time was, unlike the town, which seemed never to have learned. The town had suffered under the Hawkins brothers for so long because no one had recognized when the time to fight back had come.

But Stuartson had said that Storey was not a natural killer, and that was also true. There was a time to allow the law to do its work, and that work did not involve killing.

"Do you think we can count on this polecat getting what he deserves if we can get him back to town?" Storey said.

"I'm sure that we can," Stump said, who was seeing almost normal now. "Look down the trail."

Storey looked and saw Naomi returning in the buggy. But she wasn't alone. Carl Gary was riding along beside her, and there were several other men coming behind.

"Looks like they finally figured things out," Storey said. He didn't hold the delay against them. He had been confused for a while himself.

"I believe they have," Stump said, smiling. He had never been so glad to see his wife before.

"Looks like the jailhouse for you, Ben," Storey said, relaxing even more but still holding the knife in place.

"They won't be able to keep me in there," Ben said.

"I wouldn't bet on it," Storey told him. "I think these folks have learned a lesson."

It was late when Storey got back to the show wagon. The bodies of Dr. Stuartson and Coy Wilson had been covered with blankets, and they would be gone soon. Tal Thurman was on the way to get them.

Storey dismounted and rapped on the door at the back of the wagon.

"It's me," he said.

Louisa threw the door open and looked out.

"You're hurt," she said. "What happened?"

Storey told them what had happened as best he could. His right arm still throbbed with pain.

"I wish that Dr. Stuartson were alive to look at that arm," the Colonel said. "It may be that your shoulder is broken."

Storey thought that might be the case. "I'm more worried about the bullet wound, though," he said.

Sophia smiled. "I think we might be able to take care of that."

"Certainly," the Colonel said. "Louisa, fetch us a bottle of Miracle Oil."

Louisa handed him a bottle. "Take off your shirt," he said.

Storey began working on the buttons awkwardly with one hand, and Louisa stepped over to help him.

"I don't know about taking my shirt off in front of ladies," Storey said.

"You might as well get used to it," Louisa said.

"And what do you mean by that, young woman?" Sophia said.

Louisa looked at her mother and smiled. "Nothing," she said. She moved behind Storey and helped him as he shrugged out of the shirt.

"A nasty looking wound," the Colonel said. "But never fear. Indian Miracle Oil will do the job. It settles the stomach of man or beast, flushes the kidneys, relieves coughs, soothes catarrh—"

"I'm sure he's heard the pitch, Father," Louisa said.

"Of course, of course," the Colonel said, liberally applying his potion to the wound.

Storey gritted his teeth and tried not to flinch, but he did. He found that Louisa was holding his hand. He also found that he did not mind.

"Are you going to be with the show for a while, Mr. Storey?" the Colonel said as he inspected the wound. "It would be most difficult for us to function with neither a doctor nor a Kit Carson."

"I believe I'll stick around for a while," Storey said, smiling at Louisa. His arm was already feeling better. The Miracle Oil really was as good as Mahaffey said. Maybe his shoulder wasn't broken after all.

"I'm glad you'll be staying with us," Sophia said. "I have a feeling—"

"Never mind," the Colonel said. "I don't want to hear about it. If the next stop is anything like this one, people will begin to run when they hear we are coming into town."

He found a strip of cloth and bandaged Storey's wound.

"You may put on your shirt now," he said. "And then I think that we should all go outside and bid Dr. Stuartson a proper farewell."

Storey thought that life would be mighty strange without The Boozer around, and he realized that he was going to miss him more than he would have guessed.

The Colonel opened the door, and after a second Storey followed the others out into the moonlight.

B-2